'The lad suddide
brush before h n of
dust and swee ed.

The lighting w ers,
and because th heart
nearly stopped with gave
an enormous and noisy gasp.

The lad dropped his brush, the breath whistling
between his teeth in a gasp every bit as big as
Addy's. Then he scowled at her and rescued the
broom, beginning to try to pick up the scattered dirt
with its help.

"What do you think you're doing in here," he said, his
voice hostile . . . '

Addy has just left school, but her boring first job,
painting identical mugs at the local pottery, suddenly
becomes disturbingly exciting when she meets Lance –
an attractive student with a holiday job at the pottery.
For Lance reveals a very different kind of life to Addy
and, as the two of them discover a shared interest
in a child ghost who is said to haunt the pottery's
museum, Addy finds herself with a boyfriend for the
very first time. But could she be getting into more than
she realizes? For the ghost is not the only mystery at
the pottery . . .

*Also available by Judith Saxton,
and published by Corgi Freeway Books:*

SUMMER IN THE LAKES

CROCK OF GOLD

CROCK OF GOLD

Judith Saxton

CORGI
FREEWAY

CROCK OF GOLD

CORGI FREEWAY BOOK 0 552 525774

First publication in Great Britain

PRINTING HISTORY
Corgi Freeway edition published 1990

This book is set in 11/12pt Palatino by Chippendale Type Limited,
Otley, West Yorkshire.

Corgi Freeway Books are published by Transworld Publishers Ltd.,
61-63 Uxbridge Road, Ealing, London W5 5SA, in Australia by
Transworld Publishers (Australia) Pty. Ltd., 15-23 Helles Avenue,
Moorebank, NSW 2170, and in New Zealand by Transworld
Publishers (N.Z.) Ltd., Cnr. Moselle and Waipareira Avenues,
Henderson, Auckland.

Printed and bound in Great Britain by
Cox & Wyman Ltd, Reading

1

'Drat those lupins!' Addy muttered, as she endeavoured to push her bicycle up the garden path between straggling shrubs on one side and overgrown lupins on the other. She had been meaning to cut them back for weeks now but somehow there was always something more interesting to do. Mum ought to do it really, but she always pleaded her job made her too busy and said Addy should do it. Only now I've got a job as well, Addy told herself, virtuously flattening lupins with her front wheel and yet reluctant to tear the spikes off because they really were pretty, Mum and I should work out a rota in the house and the garden.

They never would do so though, because Addy's mother was not houseproud. Or garden-proud, for that matter. Until Gran had died two years ago the old lady had kept the garden nice, with occasional help from Addy, but now it fended for itself, as did the little end-of-terrace house. Addy was sixteen and she could not remember her mother ever weeding or tidying, any more than she could imagine her with a paintbrush in her hand.

With Gran gone, things had got a bit slack, but as Addy told herself now, pushing her bike down the narrow path at one side of the house and skirting the washing-line with its sagging burden, at least Mum wasn't the type to nag about untidiness or insist on furniture-polishing or window-cleaning. She kicked open the shed door and chained her bike to her mother's much newer machine, then heaved a sigh. She was tired after her first day's work but she arranged a smile on her face, tried to will a sparkle into her eyes. Mum had got her the job; the least she could do was pretend she had really enjoyed her day.

It hadn't been that bad, either. Just not what she had expected. She had hoped for younger workmates, not the line of middle-aged mums at the long bench with only one of them – Betty – under forty, beside Addy herself. And she had hoped for a bit more freedom to use her undoubted ability to draw and paint. Instead, she had been told to daub colour on to a design already transferred on to the white crock, and to do it quickly. She could not take her time, shade the colours, deepen the tint of a petal or change the curve of a leaf. They all had to be exactly the same – flat red poppies with black centres and a bit of green foliage.

Mum worked in the pot-bank, of course, since it was by far the biggest employer in Princeton, but she wasn't in the old workrooms of the Princeton Museum, where Addy was based. Mum was in the modern factory next door where masses of crockery was produced. In the museum you worked by hand, as they had worked over a hundred years earlier. Visitors came and went on guided tours, whispering breathily over your shoulder, telling each other to 'Look at that!' as they were hustled along.

But it was a job. She was bringing money in. And her mother, heaven knew, needed all the help she could get. She was not a good manager, and that was a kind way of putting it. The truth was that Mum had leaned on Gran whilst she was alive and had never bothered to learn the value of money. Now, she spent like a sailor until she was skint and then went on the borrow.

Addy pushed the back door open and went into the cluttered little kitchen. Her mother was not there but the swinging door into the hall was proof that she had only recently left, and as Addy crossed the room she heard a door at the top of the stairs bang shut. Mum had rushed in, dumped her shopping and hurried upstairs to the loo, leaving . . . Addy grabbed a pan of milk off the stove just before it boiled, and carried it over to the sink. There were potato peelings all over the draining board and a handful of peeled potatoes lurking in the dirty water in the bowl. No homemaker, Mum!

It was a warm evening, the July sun still strong at six o'clock, so Addy left the back door open and investigated the fridge. Two pork chops in a plastic pack and some frozen peas were all unfreezing rapidly, having probably spent the afternoon in Mum's shopping bag. All the women at the pot-bank used their dinner hour to do their shopping.

Addy was still wondering whether to put the chops under the grill when a black and white head rammed itself into the fridge; Bunty, their old cat, made an ineffectual grab at the chops as Addy smartly shut the door.

'Eat your own food,' she advised, looking round for Bunty's saucers. But they were missing. Mum hid them since Bunty could get in through the open kitchen window-light but not out again. If she got in and found food then she messed in a corner, hence the hidden cat dishes.

'Hello, love! How'd it go? Not too bad? What happened to the milk?'

Addy's mum was a natural blonde, or so she told people, though Addy knew very well that she helped nature on a bit with lemon juice when she was hard-up and a commercial hair bleach when she was in the money. But the golden-blonde hair suited the big blue eyes, the curvy figure and the scarlet-lipped smile – all things which Addy longed to own but knew she would never possess. She was small, dark and skinny, looking a good deal younger than her years, though Mum was always assuring Addy that no one believed she had a teenage daughter. Addy took this with a pinch of salt, though. It seemed like wishful thinking. Her parent was thirty-five, not exactly a child, so why should anyone think she was too young to be Addy's mother?

'It went all right,' Addy said now. Try though she might, she could not sound wildly enthusiastic but she knew her mother was unlikely to notice. You had to hit Mum over the head with a fact before she noticed it, unless it directly concerned her. 'I took your milk off. It had boiled. What was it for?'

'Custard,' her mother said, pointing vaguely in the general direction of the pantry. 'Get a packet, there's a dear. I'll see to the rest. Got you a hot meal, seeing as you've been working.'

Addy began to make the custard whilst Mum, humming to herself, scrabbled the potatoes out of the sink and into a saucepan, turned on the gas, put the chops under the grill, turned that gas on too and then lit a match, waving it wildly between the grill and the ring beneath the potatoes. Not surprisingly the gas lit with a *whump* which made Addy leap a mile and caused Bunty to hiss and fluff out her tail.

'Got to get a move on,' Mum said, looking surprised and rather offended. You could tell she thought the gas had behaved unreasonably. 'I'm off out this evening – it's that feller in Despatch. I said I thought he was interested, remember? I'm going to wear my pink jeans with the white voile blouse and the gold chains. We're going to the Troc.'

The Trocadero was a very large pub with a dance-floor. Addy had never been inside but her mother, she knew, went there often.

'Oh. Have a nice time, then. You'll be late, I suppose?'

'Lateish, I dare say. Damn, where did I hide Bunty's saucers this morning?' Mum frowned, then dived into the oven. Her voice floated back to Addy, muffled, echoing. 'Why d'you ask? You don't mind being alone in the house all of a sudden, do you?'

'I don't mind,' Addy said resignedly. 'I could go out as well, I suppose.'

She could go and see Diane, her best friend from school. The trouble was, Addy had left school to become one of the world's workers,

11

and Di was going on to Tech to take A levels and a Business Studies course. It had changed their relationship and Addy did not want to go rushing round to Di's. It would look as though she had failed to make any friends at work, and even if this were true – which it was – she did not want to admit defeat too soon.

'Yes, you go out,' Mum said encouragingly, putting the cat's saucers on the floor. 'Meet anyone nice at work? A lad? But you aren't interested, are you!'

'They're all women in the paint-room,' Addy said, begging the second part of the question. 'They're all quite old, as well.'

'Pity,' her mother said absently. She crouched by Bunty, tickling the cat's ears as she began to eat. 'No lads at all?' She pushed at the thick, bouncing curls on her shoulders in a gesture which Addy knew well and then stood up, glancing at her reflection in the windowpane. 'Wouldn't do for me; I like a few fellers around.'

'Well, I saw one . . .' Addy began

'Really? Nice, is he? Chat you up, did he?'

'I only saw him, we didn't speak,' Addy said sullenly. It made her feel so inadequate when Mum talked about lads as though she thought her daughter was peculiar not to have a string of them dogging her heels. 'He's not in the paint-room, he's probably a student doing a holiday job.'

'Oh, a student.' Her mother lost interest at once, clearly considering a student did not count as a feller. 'Well, chuck, if you want a date I could arrange something, now you're working. A feller from my side of the factory – we could double-date, that 'ud be a laugh, eh?'

'No thanks,' Addy said, knowing she sounded cross but unable to do anything about it. Why couldn't she have a mother like Diane's, a sensible, plump person with a job on school dinners and absolutely no interest in men? Di's mother scarcely spoke to her husband so far as Addy could see, except to ask him if he wanted more potatoes. When girls at school envied her her youthful mother, said that Lila Bates looked more like Addy's sister, she always had to bite her tongue not to say tartly that it was no fun to feel that her mother had got there first and intended to stay there. Mum knew more about pop music than most sixteen year olds, more about lads, more about fashion, and she never let Addy forget it, either. And in an odd sort of way it made Addy equally responsible for the house, the cat, their budget, because now that Gran was dead Mum made it plain that she was only an adult on the outside. On the inside, she was every bit as young as her daughter.

'All right then, no double-dates,' Mum said, her temporary interest in Addy subsiding. She poked hopefully at the potatoes, though they could not possibly be ready yet, and reached under the grill, flicking the chops over though they were still half-raw. Addy could see that her mother wanted to abandon the meal, rush upstairs, bath, prink and titivate. If I was blonde . . . or prettier, not so skinny. . . life would be easier for us both because I'd share her feelings, Addy thought desperately. But as it was . . .

'You go and get changed; I'll finish cooking,' she said resignedly. 'I'll probably stay at home this evening, after all.'

Her mother, after a token refusal, rushed off and presently rejoined Addy for the meal. She was carefully made-up, perfumed and dressed. They carried their plates into the front room and switched on the telly. One of the soaps was on, and familiar figures crossed and recrossed the small screen. Addy's mother was immediately absorbed, eating with her eyes never leaving the flickering picture before her. Addy ate her food whilst she, too, eyed the screen. But she saw only with her inward eye; she was replaying her day.

Addy's place on the bench was between Susan Fryer and Betty Smith. Susan was in her late forties and Betty was twenty, so she found Betty easier to talk to, though she was obsessed with lads. But she was kind enough, commiserating with Addy over being stuck with the older women and assuring her that she might well get a transfer to the modern factory once she'd been there a while.

'Besides, some of the visitors are quite nice,' she said, giving Addy a roguish glance out of her bold, dark eyes. 'Some of em's lads! I'm a trainee guide, me, which gets me out of here now and then.'

Poor Addy had forced a smile and suppressed a shriek: it was Mum all over again. If you didn't like lads there was something radically wrong with you. When would she ever escape it? And then Susan put her oar in.

'Lila Bates's daughter, aren't you?' she had said, peering at Addy over her pink-framed glasses. 'I'd never have thought it.'

'It's the clothes,' Betty said quickly. She turned to Addy. 'Did you choose 'em yourself?'

'Not exactly,' Addy said guardedly. She had no intention of admitting that she had let her mother select her clothing for years, on the grounds that since Addy herself was not interested, Mum would just get 'something suitable'. Indeed, it was only very recently that Addy had begun to resent the skimpy, dull skirts and dresses, realizing that other girls of her age wore far more exciting stuff.

'I'll come shopping with you when you get paid, if you like,' Betty suggested. 'Your mum's a good dresser, no one would deny that.'

'Good? Gaudy!' Susan said and shrieked with laughter, then leaned across and told Addy she was only joking whilst Betty, rather affronted, whispered to Addy that you couldn't expect the older ones to appreciate a bit of style and fashion.

'Your mum always looks crisp and colourful,' Betty explained. 'She's got a flair for what looks good on her; you'll likely be the same.'

Addy agreed, smiled, painted another poppy and some more leaves, pushed the mug to the front of her bench to be dried and reached for the next thick white mug.

The morning dragged, there was no doubt about that. But at last it was half-past twelve and Beryl Hardwick, their supervisor, rang a handbell and headed for the door, reminding Addy, over her shoulder, that she would not be needed in the paint-room for an hour.

Addy headed for the door with the others, at first conscious only of joy at her release but wondering, as soon as she reached the cobbled yard around which the workrooms were grouped, what she should do. She had not thought about having a dinner hour so had neither money nor a packed meal, but at least she could wander round outside in the sunshine and think her own thoughts.

She picked up her school blazer and forced it on – it was a tight fit – over the grey skirt and cream blouse, whilst her stomach growled peevish disapproval at this sudden departure from routine. Usually she had a school dinner or chips at this time. She really should have thought, but since she had no intention of admitting to anyone that she had no money, she took a hunted look round and then headed for the museum itself, where the exhibition of pottery was located.

The women who had brought sandwiches were clustered on the low wall which separated the car-park from the factory and museum grounds. Others were streaming out into the roadway, intent on shopping or going out for chips. There was a canteen in the modern factory where workers got a cheap meal, but if you were employed in the old workrooms you could go to the snack bar upstairs in the museum, and get something there at a special price. So when her workmates saw Addy going into the museum they would assume she was going up there, or so Addy reasoned, slipping out of the sunshine and into the cool darkness of the museum foyer. She would stay there for a little while and then emerge into the sunshine and everyone would assume she had eaten upstairs.

Betty shouted to her, something about walking round the shops when she'd had her dinner, but

16

Addy pretended not to hear. She let the door swing shut behind her and decided, on impulse, to have a proper look round. As a child she had loved the Princeton Museum but had not been there for years. Now she would take advantage of working next door, in the old workrooms, and admire the exhibits once again.

The museum was clearly closed to the public since the foyer was unlit and the long desk unmanned, but that, if anything, added to the fun of her sudden decision. She was able to wander at will, in and out of the long, white-painted rooms, hanging over the glass cases and marvelling at the beauty of the china displayed in them.

It was a first-rate exhibition. Colours, shapes and designs swam before Addy's enchanted eyes until she was so full of the wonder of it that even her empty stomach stopped reminding her of its hollowness. There was china which had been made in this very museum when it had been the only factory on the site; the pieces ranged from the very earliest items to the sort of thing her mother and her colleagues made today. There were rooms of porcelain made in China, in Japan and in Korea, some of it centuries old, some relatively new. Addy saw the delicacy of blue and white ware, eggshell fine, shapes that cried out to be touched, textures so fine, so rare, that the artist in her swooned with envy. It was things like this which she had dreamed of helping to create when she had applied for a job in the pottery, not thick white mugs and flat red poppies!

She might have forgotten all about the time and her job had it not been for the lad.

He was in the delft-room, so called because of the display of delft china in the first two or three cases, and he must have been in the far corner for Addy did not see him when she first entered. Then a movement caught her eyes, she looked up from a display of teapots, and the lad suddenly came into view, pushing a wide brush before him, his eyes fixed on the small burden of dust and sweetpapers which his broom had collected.

The lighting was off in this room as in all the others, and because the lad was making no noise Addy's heart nearly stopped with the sudden surprise, and she gave an enormous and noisy gasp.

The lad dropped his brush, the breath whistling between his teeth in a gasp every bit as big as Addy's. Then he scowled at her and rescued the broom, beginning to try to pick up the scattered dirt with its help.

'What do you think you're doing in here?' he said, his voice hostile. 'We're closed – it's lunchtime. You damned nearly made me put the broom through a glass case.'

'What are *you* doing, then?' Addy said, bristling. 'If it's closed, why are you sweeping up and not having your dinner? Anyway, I work here, I can come in whenever I like.'

'Oh? I haven't seen you about before.'

They stared at each other, both hostile now, and then, suddenly, the lad grinned.

'I'm new here, actually, the name's Lance Peterson. How do you do?'

Addy smiled too, though rather reluctantly. They had both scared each other, and she might as well tell him who she was since she had every intention of spending quite a lot of time in the museum.

'I'm Adelaide Bates – Addy, my friends call me. I'm in the paint-room . . . you know, we paint the china just like they did in the eighteen sixties.'

He nodded. 'Yes, of course, that's why we haven't met. I've not been in the working part of the museum yet, only in this bit. I'm doing the old glass-polishing, floor-sweeping bit over the summer vacation. You doing a holiday job too?'

'No. I'm working full time,' Addy said. 'It's pretty dull right now, but it should get better.'

He nodded, then began to sweep again, neatly skirting round Addy and speaking over his shoulder.

'I couldn't do this for the rest of my life, but then it takes all sorts. Cheerio, see you around.'

He and his broom disappeared out of the door through which Addy had just come. Not knowing quite why, Addy found that she was annoyed and somehow on the defensive all over again. Why did he conclude that she could paint china for the rest of her life, just because it was a full-time job? He was a snob, that's what it was . . . Oh, he couldn't possibly be bored just to earn *money*, he had to be interested in what he was doing; that sort of snob.

Addy walked along to the next case and peered inside, but the beautiful delftware had lost its appeal. She could feel a flush creeping up into her cheeks at the thought of that lad's casual assumption that 'it takes all sorts'. So he thought they were different sorts, did he? Well, so they were . . . he was an idle student, doing a job to fend off the boredom of doing nothing, whilst Addy worked because she needed the money, and . . . and . . .

The job! She needed the money and she was going to be late back on her very first day!

Addy flew out of the museum, across the yard and up the rickety steps into the paint-room. She was not late, everyone was pulling out chairs, reaching for china, sorting out their paints. Betty was just behind her, out of breath, a trifle reproachful.

'You never came out,' she said, sliding into her seat. 'I shouted after you . . . didn't you hear?'

'Sorry,' muttered Addy, skirting an outright lie. 'I went round the museum, it was great.'

'Oh, yeah? But it's closed, for dinner.'

'Yes, but it isn't locked or anything. I say, Betty, who's the lad who works there?'

'A lad? In there? News to me,' Betty said. She painted a poppy lopsided but no one seemed to mind. 'Oh, they usually have someone in for the summer . . . tall chap? Brown hair?'

'Ye-es,' Addy decided, having thought it over. He had dark hair with light strands on the top where the sun had caught it, and although he was tall and quite thin he looked tough as well. Rather nice, in fact. His blue jeans had been quite new-looking, his shirt crisp and recently ironed. Seeing him again in her mind's eye, Addy realized that he was what her mother would have called *very fanciable*.

'Oh, aye. Don't know his name but he's rather tasty,' Betty said frankly. 'Puts my Ted in the shade for looks.'

Addy mumbled something. She had heard a good deal about 'my Ted' already and did not want to hear more.

'Saw him in the museum, did you?' Betty asked, reaching for the next mug. 'Fancy a bit of that, then?'

'No,' Addy said baldly. Did the girl think of nothing else? 'I just wondered if you knew why he was working during the dinner hour? He gave me an awful fright, marching out from behind a display case when I thought I was the only person in there.'

Betty shrugged, sloshing paint. 'Probably wants to leave at half-four. If you work through your dinner hour you can take the time off and leave early.'

'Oh,' Addy said. 'He could do it often, then, if he wanted?'

She did not want to walk into him again when she was enjoying a quiet wander round the museum, but forewarned was forearmed. Next time she would check where Lance Peterson – silly name – was before entering any of the rooms suddenly.

'Ye-es, only the bosses don't like us leaving early more than once or twice a week. It messes other people around, you see. But if you don't fancy him, what does it matter where he spends his dinner hour?'

'It doesn't, I just wondered,' Addy said vaguely. 'When do we get paid, Betty? Would you really come shopping with me when I've got some money?'

'Sure,' Betty said easily. 'Tell you what, Beryl was saying someone would have to take you

21

round the workshops so that you know how the crocks are made, the whole process. I'm a trainee guide so I could take you, if you like. Beryl's ever so good, she'll give us an hour or so off to do the tour and if we get a move on, get round sharpish, we could win ourselves a bit of extra time for shopping. Kill two birds with one stone.'

'Lovely,' Addy said, blobbing on red paint. Betty was all right really. The job was all right, too. And one day . . . one day she would paint fine china freehand and use her artistic skills, which would show that self-satisfied Lance Peterson that she was not content to be stuck in the mud of the paint-room, whatever he might think.

2

For the next four days Addy continued to paint poppies, chat to the other women on her bench, go around with Betty at dinner-time, and to see nothing whatsoever of Lance. But then Beryl remembered that Addy had not yet done the rounds of the other workrooms and told Betty to do her a private tour so that she could see how the mugs and plates, cups and saucers which she decorated were made, fired and glazed.

Betty pointed out that it would be rather nice if she and Addy could do the tour about an hour before dinner, but Beryl said she knew a trick worth two of that.

'I don't mind giving you time off to tour the workshops,' Beryl said, frowning at Betty. 'But not so's you can rush through it at top speed and then out and spend your brass in the firm's time. Off you go, the pair of you, and tek it all in, young Addy. One day they may want you to take parties round, like Betty does.'

They can want, Addy thought crossly, whilst being polite and thanking Beryl for letting them go. She had got used to the tourists but she could never bring herself to exchange backchat with them as the others did. The thought of taking parties round was terrifying, though she knew perfectly well that Beryl was joking. Everyone knew that you only guided parties if you wanted to, because there was nothing worse than being taken round by someone so tongue-tied that they mumbled and blushed all the time.

The money was better for guiding, Betty said, but right now Addy thought her mother ought to be quite grateful enough to her for working here at all. It was so boring, dabbing paint on mugs day after day, but at least she was earning and there was no doubt it would be nice to have some money of her own.

Things at home were difficult. Mum had a new boyfriend, the feller in Despatch having come up trumps, so Addy found herself alone after work most evenings. She could have gone round to Di's, of course, but she didn't want to do that until she had her new clothes. She was wondering whether she could get away with pink jeans, or whether they would simply draw attention to her lack of curves, when Betty began her tour, pushed open the first door and started talking.

'It all starts here, in that gutter with the watery stuff running through. That's the slip. Clay and water, which runs along here, goes into the sausage-machine there, and comes out the other end as the sort of clay you can make pots with. That's how it all starts.'

Addy nodded. The machinery which carried the clay powder and water – the slip – to the sausage machine was too noisy for talking, but it was fascinating to see the machines clanking away, with men working just as they had worked more than a hundred years earlier. The whole place was a living, working slice out of the nineteenth century and to go through it was just like stepping back in time.

It was impossible, of course, to recreate the conditions under which the workers, many of them small children, had made the pots but instead, photographs and drawings of the youngsters, together with their stories, were reproduced and enlarged upon the walls, so that when you went into a room you saw what the children did, were told how they did it, and then read of their sufferings as the result of such work.

They were in the turning-room when the door opened and a head poked round it. It smiled at them. It was Lance.

'Hello, girls,' he said cheerfully. 'Mind if I join you? I'm taking a party of schoolkids round later, with Eva, so I want to see how it's done.'

Betty bridled, but smiled as well, winking at Addy.

'This was a private do, just for Addy,' she said. 'Never mind, I dare say one more won't hurt. What do you say, Addy? You two haven't met, I suppose?'

Addy said nothing but Lance was more forth-coming.

'We exchanged a few words in the museum earlier in the week,' he said. 'Go on then, what happened in the turning-room?'

'The children in here worked a twelve-hour day or longer, and a six-day week,' Betty said briskly. 'The worst thing was, though, they didn't usually live long. The turners took the finished pots to be fired and brought 'em back, so they were in the biscuit oven for half their working day, where the heat rose to a hundred and thirty degrees, and in the icy yard as they crossed back to the turning-room, here, where the temperature was around forty degrees. Young lungs couldn't stand it, so lots of 'em died.'

Addy moved over to the wall to examine the photographs, pointedly keeping her back to Lance. How annoying to have him pushing in on her private tour of the workrooms, and then to monopolize Betty, as he undoubtedly would. He must like Betty, who was pretty and bouncy. Well, if he wanted to run after Betty, let him, but he shouldn't muscle in on her conducted tour just for that!

'Hard luck on the little turners,' Lance murmured. 'Good job you two don't work in the turning-room.'

'No one works here now, they don't take things that far,' Betty said, smiling at him. 'It's just the pots and so on now, the tools they used. But kids died in the paint-room as well, from the fumes coming off the paint, and they used all sorts in the paint in those days as well. Oh aye, me and Addy here wouldn't have seen old age, I don't suppose.'

'Oh, Addy's old as the hills already, aren't you, Addy?' Lance said, turning to grin at her. 'She spends her dinner hour in the museum. Very serious!'

'I don't,' Addy squeaked indignantly. 'I went in there once . . . but not any more. I wouldn't want to scare you stiff again.'

'Scare *me* stiff?' Lance turned to Betty. 'Honestly, you'd have thought I was Dracula, the jump she gave when she saw me.'

'She probably thought you were a ghost,' Betty said, smiling from one to the other. 'Heaven knows, with all those little kids dying before their tenth birthday, the place could be stiff with ghosts.'

'Stiff with stiffs,' Lance said. 'What's next?'

'This here's the dipping-room. More died in the dipping-room than anywhere,' Betty said, with a touch of relish, Addy thought. 'See, the dippers were kids who brought the biscuitware through for dipping and then shelved it. It was the dip itself which was so dangerous, though of course they mostly never realized it until it was too late. It were full of awful things: lead, soda, even arsenic. And biscuitware's rough, as you know, so it thinned the skin on the kids' fingers, making it even easier for the dip to soak into their bloodstreams. And then they'd eat their snap without washing their hands, because no one knew it was poisonous so they didn't provide water for 'em to wash with. So they ate the dip and all. Dip's glaze, of course,' she added.

'This one died at only twelve years old,' Addy said, pointing to a photograph of a cheerful-looking little girl with dimples and a front tooth missing. 'Isn't it sadder, somehow, when you can see their faces? It says underneath that she took her younger brother's place in the dipping-room, because he was sickly. Then she died, poor little thing.'

'It says here that some of the children liked being in the pot-bank better than at home, because

27

they weren't beaten here,' Lance exclaimed, reading from a caption further along the wall. 'It just goes to show, doesn't it? I wonder when they stopped using child labour?'

'Oh, quite soon after the fifties, I guess,' Betty said. 'Now we'll go along to the bottle kilns; you can see how the ware was fired once it had been through the glazing.'

She led the way out into the courtyard once more. The museum was one side of the square, the still-operational workrooms where the painting, dipping and so on were done were on another two sides, and the fourth and last side was open, with the bottle kilns themselves standing well back from the main buildings and surrounded now by grass, weeds and wild shrubs of gorse and broom. There were only two kilns still standing, one very old and neglected, the other renovated so that visitors could see how a kiln had once operated.

'In the fifties they used the kilns all the time,' Betty said, joining a queue of visitors and beckoning Addy and Lance to join her. 'Today we use electric ovens, of course, but in this kiln they've got heaps of plastic coal and under that there's a real working oven, which we use to bake the ware we make over here, so that the visitors can see the whole procedure.'

'It's jolly interesting, but I'm off,' Lance said, indicating the queue. 'Sorry, girls, but I've got work to do!'

He left with a cheery wave but Addy said crossly: 'I think he's a conceited twerp! As if we didn't have work to do! Do you still think he's nice, Betty?'

'Scrumptious,' Betty said promptly. 'Lovely smooth, tanned skin, dark blue eyes . . . nice bum, an' all!'

Addy snorted. The queue inched forward. But interesting though the kiln was, the sparkle seemed to have gone out of the tour, and Addy and her companion merely peeped inside before hurrying back to the paint-room.

'Now we'll get paid,' Betty said gleefully, as they rejoined their workmates. 'Then we'll go shopping, young Addy!'

'We go in pairs to be paid, so that there's always plenty painting for the visitors,' Betty informed Addy as the two of them put down their brushes and made for the door. 'I used to go as a third, with Susan and Meggie; nice to have someone me own age to chat with.'

Addy returned some light answer, but secretly she was flattered. She was a good four years younger than Betty, but she was beginning to see that she and the other girl could get along quite well when they had to, though Betty's obsession with lads still made Addy uneasy. But right now, all Betty was obsessed with was money and since Addy felt just the same, this was fine by her.

'Where are we going?' she asked presently, however, as Betty headed for the five-barred gate leading into the modern factory. 'Don't we get paid here?'

'No. For some reason accounts are done over in the modern factory and so we go over there. Never mind, it's a nice little walk in fine weather, though it's awful in the winter, when it's wet or snowy. All our admin staff are there too, because there just isn't room for them in the old part of the place – it's all taken up with the museum, the curator's office and the snack bar.'

Accordingly, the two girls walked across the car-park and into the square, ugly, modern building next door. They went in through a side door, up a flight of stairs and found themselves in another world.

'Soft lighting, carpets, lots of plants and flowers,' Addy breathed as they got to the head of the stairs and crossed a large reception area. 'Why so smart?'

'Oh, they sell our ware all over the world, so this is to impress customers,' Betty told her. 'First door on the right, chuck.'

Addy opened the door cautiously, to find herself in a very large room indeed with a long counter and four queues of people waiting. Betty nudged her over to one of them.

'It's old-fashioned, but it's how we've always been paid, I think,' she said as they joined the queue. 'Man to man, like this. In the old days, of course, the money was paid to the foreman, who handed it on to the workers, sometimes fairly and sometimes not. So when they modernized they did it like this and they've stuck to it, though lots of workers these days get a cheque paid into a bank account. Some folk grumble, but there's advantages. If you don't understand something on your pay-slip you just ask, straight out, and someone on the counter will explain it to you.'

Addy edged forward with the rest of the queue. She took her envelope, stood to one side to open it and check the contents and then rejoined Betty. The two of them were about to leave the room when the man who had just paid them called out.

'Adelaide Bates?'

Addy turned.

'Yes? That's me.'

'Would you go along to Mr Braithwaite, in Personnel? It's three doors further along the corridor, on the right-hand side. There's a form or something you should have signed.'

'Oh . . . right now?'

'Yes, he said to get you to go along right away.'

Addy turned to Betty.

'Must I? I mean it's nearly dinner-time and we were going shopping!'

'It probably won't take a tick. I'll wait for you in the paint-room,' Betty said consolingly. 'I'll be eating my snap, then if you can eat yours quick we'll go straight out.'

'Oh, all right,' Addy sighed. Outside the door, the two of them turned and went their separate ways. Addy did not have to count doors, in fact, since the third door on the right said PERSONNEL, and under that, W.G. Braithwaite. She knocked on the door, then opened it and stuck her head into the room.

'Umm . . .'

The man sitting behind the desk was square-looking, with heavy, horn-rimmed glasses, thick, oily black hair parted slightly right of centre and fleshy pink lips. He gave Addy a quick, jerky glance and then began ferreting through the papers on his desk.

'Ah . . . Adelaide Bates? Yes, yes . . . there's a form here somewhere which should have been filled in when you were interviewed, but I was away . . . someone slipped up . . . if I can just lay my hands on it . . .'

The phone rang, sharply. Mr Braithwaite sighed, frowned, and picked up the receiver, then clattered it down again looking even more annoyed. It was not the phone which had rung, it appeared, but an intercom on the other side of the desk. Mr Braithwaite depressed a key and said, still crossly, 'Yes?'

'Got it, Walter!'

The voice spoke clearly, jubilantly almost. Mr Braithwaite shot a look at Addy, cleared his throat and answered the unseen voice.

'Ah . . . good, good. I've a young person with me, waiting for the form so she can sign it . . . I'll just pop round and fetch it.'

He took his finger off the key and came round the desk, smiling distractedly at Addy.

'There . . . it wasn't on my desk after all. I won't be a moment . . . if you'll be good enough to wait here until I come back . . . ?'

Addy, still only halfway across the room, retreated to the door and held it open for him, then stood by it, as though she would wait in the corridor. But in fact, as soon as he had bustled out of sight, she returned to the room. It was rather nice to see how the other half lived, she decided, taking a good look at the expensive silver antique inkwell, the photographs in elaborate frames, and the leather binding on the blotter and around the desk itself. Highly daring, she picked up one of the photographs and looked at the picture of a fat, spotty child and was just carefully replacing it when a voice spoke right in her ear, nearly causing her to have a heart attack on the spot.

'It's foolproof I tell you; it can't go wrong. If we get the heat right and Jacko can rustle up transport then we'll all be millionaires!'

Addy's heart gave a huge thump and she stared wildly round her, but the room was empty save for herself.

'Millionaires? There must be a deal of it, then!'

That was a different voice, deeper, with a strong Scottish accent. And now Addy saw where the voices were coming from. The intercom was still switched on; the key must have stuck down when Mr Braithwaite had taken his finger off it, so she was hearing a conversation coming from another room. A respectable girl would knock the key up again, because this was eavesdropping, but although Addy moved nearer to the desk, she had not touched the key when the voice spoke again.

'We-ell, yes, but it weighs heavy, of course. We've been fetching it over for a while, now, so it's mounted up. And this way, don't you see, there's no chance of anyone being fingered. It's absolutely legal, that's the beauty of it.'

Another voice broke in whilst Addy, frowning, was still trying to make sense of what had been said.

'He's right, Ned. Once it's unmarked it's all absolutely legal and above board. Are you on?'

Without thinking twice, Addy leaned across and switched the key up, cutting off the speakers. She would have known that rich, plummy voice anywhere – it was Mr Braithwaite! And what-ever the conversation had been about, she was suddenly sure that she could be in very hot water if the men ever discovered they had been overheard. She ran across the room on tiptoe, out through the open door and into the corridor outside. She was leaning on the white wall, apparently examining her pay envelope, when Mr Braithwaite hoved in view once more, coming from her left. He was breathing heavily, as though he had been hurrying, and looked surprised to see her.

'Hello, what can I . . . ah yes, it's Miss Bates, isn't it? Yes, come about a form.'

'You went to get me one,' Addy said, highly daring. She was sure he had been doing no such thing, especially since he did not have a form in his hand, but apparently he had an answer for this, too.

'That's right, but the member of staff who holds such things is on his lunch hour. I'll send the form down to the paint-room some time this afternoon. Now you run off, my dear, and get your meal.'

Addy obeyed, hurrying out of the building and down into the car-park first and then the courtyard. But once back at the paint-room, a disappointment awaited her. Beryl sat at one of the tables, placidly knitting between bites of sandwich, and she looked up as Addy hurried into the room.

'Oh, Addy, love, I've a message for you. Ted's got an hour off, so he came round and Bet went off with him. She's ever so sorry, she says, but you can go shopping with her Monday, if you like.'

Monday! No way, thought Addy crossly. She wanted her new clothes for the weekend. Wha

34

a nuisance . . . but she could always shop by herself. She looked at her watch and despite Mr Braithwaite's delaying tactics she still had nearly her whole hour left, so she took her blazer from the hooks by the door and thanked Beryl for the message, then set off. She would hurry down to Mates, where they sold cheap clothes for teenagers, and get something, just some jeans and a shirt, then she could really go to town on Saturday, with Diane.

She was crossing the courtyard again, hurrying now, when a voice hailed her. Addy stopped with an inward groan. It really was not her lucky day, she would never reach the shops at this rate. She turned and there was Lance, leaning on a yard broom and smiling at her.

'Hey . . . Addy! Going somewhere? Spending your loot?'

'Yes . . . just a bit of it,' Addy said. 'Sorry, can't stop.'

She was actually going out of the gates when Lance caught her arm, slowing if not stopping her.

'I'll come . . . I want to buy some Y-fronts myself.'

Addy was about to invite him, frostily, to get stuffed and what was more to do it alone, when the conversation she had inadvertently listened to crossed her mind once more. It was intriguing, there was no doubt about that and Lance, being as new to this place as she was, might perhaps be interested as well.

'All right, we'll walk up to town together,' she said, therefore. 'I'm going to Mates to get some jeans.'

35

'Fine. Where's your pal?'

The scales fell from Addy's eyes. So it was Betty he was after! Well, he'd get a disappointment then, if they happened to meet Betty and her Ted. But she could still tell him what she'd overheard.

'Betty's gone out with someone,' she said. 'Get paid today, did you?'

'Uh huh. Where else would I get money for Y-fronts?'

'From Mummy and Daddy?' Addy suggested, stung by his casual tone and so imitating his accent, which was south of England rather than north, like Addy's own. 'Do they buy your clothes?'

He had been strolling beside her, hands thrust into pockets, his general attitude casual, easy. Now he stiffened and looked down at her, his mouth tightening.

'No, they don't,' he said, with an edge to his voice. 'What makes you think they might?'

'Well, if you're a student, I suppose you're still their responsibility,' Addy said uncertainly. She wished she hadn't been quite so sharp and, seeing him still frowning, shook her head at herself, then tried to put matters right. 'I'm sorry, it was a stupid thing to say. I'd have been mad at you if you'd said it to me. The thing is, I want to ask you something about being paid this morning and I was only trying to start the conversation going in the right direction, if you see what I mean.'

'It's all right,' Lance said. He gave a long sigh. 'I guess we're both a bit touchy. Go on then, ask me about being paid.'

'Well, when I went to get my money . . .'

36

Addy told him the whole story, right down to the moment when Mr Braithwaite had come back down the corridor, still without her form. Then she eyed Lance hopefully.

'What does it all mean, do you suppose? If he hadn't said that about being millionaires I'd just have thought they were talking about pots or crocks . . . but you don't think of china making people that rich, do you?'

'Whoever they are, they're up to something, probably something crooked,' Lance agreed. 'Intriguing! It's a pity it all took place in the modern factory though. I don't suppose there's much chance of our ever finding out what they're up to. Hey, wait a moment! Did you say one of the guys had a Scottish accent?'

'Yes. I think his name was Ned.'

'Ned! Then we've got a chance, because the guy who fires the kilns for our handmade pottery is a Scot called Ned.'

'Really? And the kilns are fired two days a week, aren't they? Can you keep an eye on him when they're firing, do you think? I don't suppose there's anything in it, but I'd love to know what little swindle they're hatching.'

'I'll have a go,' Lance agreed. 'Here's Mates. Come on, we might as well stay together here, I don't plan on trying on my Y-fronts.'

It was a new experience for Addy to go clothes shopping at all, so going with a lad was entirely novel and, rather to her surprise, fun as well. They bought his Y-fronts with a bit of horsing around over the silly ones with writing on, but he got plain white in the end, and then they went into the jeans section and here Lance was really quite

37

helpful, pointing out the various different types, telling Addy that regardless of how she felt she really should try them on, and then assuring her that the dark ones would probably last longer than the stone-washed, as well as going far better with the white and lemon T-shirts she had chosen.

They left the shop on really good terms with each other, their purchases in the dark brown bags with silver writing on, and hurried back to the museum. At the gates Lance, going a bit red, suggested that they might spend some time together over the weekend.

'We could talk about the millionaire business, try to get to the bottom of it,' he suggested diffidently. 'And there's another matter I'd like to tell you about . . . only we don't get much time as a rule.'

Addy knew she was going every bit as red as he, but she agreed that it might be fun to meet, just for an hour or so. She wondered whether she should suggest Betty came along as well, then knew she couldn't possibly say such a thing since they had both already agreed that the fewer people to know about the eaves-dropping the better. And besides, three was a difficult number.

'When, though?' she said, as they strolled across the courtyard. 'Saturday? Or Sunday?'

'Tell you what, meet me for a coffee in the Coffee Bean on Saturday at eleven and we'll talk about it. Are you on?'

'I'm on,' Addy said, face now on fire; a number of the girls were sunning themselves in the yard, waiting for the fateful hour of one-thirty to strike. Several were staring interestedly towards

Lance and Addy. They probably thought she was being asked out . . . and I am, Addy thought, awestruck. Having coffee with a guy is a date!

'See you, then,' Lance said. He raised a hand, then loped through the double doors into the museum. Addy heard the clock striking the half-hour and joined the throng waiting to go back up the stairs and into the paint-room. Wait till Betty heard that she was having coffee tomorrow with Lance Peterson!

3

Addy hurried out of work that evening and rushed up to Tesco, where she bought her mother a present before hurrying home. She knew better than to arrive home with her first wage packet, clothing she had bought herself, and nothing for Mum. And she was glad she had got the things, because her mother's transparent delight was a pleasure to watch. She said all the right things, gobbled the chocolates whilst watching television that same evening, and wore the crystal drop earrings immediately, pulling her big plastic ones out and replacing them at once, her mouth smiling and pouting as she tried different expressions to show off her new possessions. She was a nice person to give a present to, Addy acknowledged to herself. Her delight was unfeigned. So they settled down to an evening at home feeling very pleased with one another.

But next morning a shadow was cast on this togetherness by Addy's expressed intent to go shopping for some more clothes.

'Now, madam, I know you earned the money but we need it; we've got to eat,' her mother said at once. 'I thought you'd hand your packet over and

I'd give you back pocket money for your dinners and that. I'll buy you any clothes you need.'

'Mum, it's not eighteen fifty in this house, even if it is at work,' Addy protested, half laughing. Surely Mum could not be serious? Addy expected to pay for her keep, of course, but not to hand her wage packet over. Her mother could not believe she would do that!

She was wrong. Lila Bates had never considered that her quiet little daughter would expect to keep her money and it took a lot of stubbornness on Addy's part before her mother sighed, shrugged, and said in that case, since she herself put all of her wages into the house bar a tenner, Addy could do the same.

'No,' Addy said firmly. 'That's not fair, Mum, and it's not really true, either. You go out a lot and have heaps of clothes and make-up and stuff like that. I'll give you a tenner if you like and you can see how far it'll go.'

'A tenner! Have you any idea what things cost? There's the rent, the rates, taxes, food . . .'

'I'll buy my own food,' Addy said cheekily and was sorry when, for a moment, her mother looked confounded, all the wind taken out of her sails by the unexpected remark. 'Look,' Addy finished desperately, 'I'll give you half. Is that fair?'

'It'll have to do, I suppose,' her mother said after rather a long pause. 'I'll do some sums. And I'll come shopping with you, just to make sure you don't spend your money on cheap rubbish.'

Addy shook her head, tightening her lips. She had every intention of spending as little money as possible so her clothing, of necessity, would be fairly cheap, but Addy knew her mother really feared that her daughter might buy expensive stuff and need more money than the half she had claimed.

'I'll be better alone,' she said firmly, and then added that she was meeting a friend for coffee anyway, though she did not intend to divulge that it was a male friend. You could never tell with Mum, she might be delighted or scaldingly indifferent or she might turn up at the coffee shop to have a nose around. Better to say nothing at this stage.

And in fact Addy was lucky, because she was in the bathroom first next day, then actually wheeling her bicycle down the garden path whilst her mother was still in the shower so the question of being accompanied did not arise.

'Addy!' wailed a voice from the bathroom as she clicked the gate open. 'Addy . . . fetch me up a clean towel!'

Delaying tactics; Mum was famous for them. But Addy told herself that she had not heard and cycled happily away into the sunny morning. Now for some real clothes-buying – and she was wearing her jeans and a white T-shirt to show Lance that she was a perfectly normal teenager really and could look good in something other than an old school blouse and skirt.

She went first to Diane's shop; Di was working at the local newsagent's. Addy was full of her new clothes, new job and new – tentative – friendship with A Lad. The capitals, she knew, would be Di's, because her friend had had a helpless crush for six months on a lad called Springer and would be intrigued that slow Addy had actually gone one better and got herself a date.

But here she was wrong. Diane told her, starry-eyed, that she, too, was going out that evening with a lad.

'Springer's taking me to see the new film at the Odeon,' she said proudly. 'Imagine that, Addy – it seems he noticed me ages ago, he's just been biding his time.'

Diane had black, bouncy curls, blue eyes and freckles. Addy knew her friend was enchantingly pretty and now, it seemed, Diane was beginning to realize it as well. She was pleased for Diane, of course, but a little sorry for herself. Life would change for both of them if they managed to acquire boyfriends . . . but then life *keeps* changing, Addy reminded herself. It's good that it does, not bad. It'll give us more to talk about when we do manage to meet up. And anyway, Lance would not become a boyfriend, he wasn't interested in her like that, he merely wanted a friend, as she did.

Still, she went into the coffee shop with a light step and her head well up, hoping that some of her old class at school would be around to see her and Lance together. It would just teach them that you could be interested in painting and drawing and still be attractive to the lads!

Lance was late, which was bad, but at least he apologized for it, sitting down opposite her with a thump, out of breath, and explaining that he had had the devil's own job to park his car.

'I've got a key to the museum car-park, for weekends,' he explained, having ordered coffee and doughnuts for two. 'Only I went and forgot it, so I hung around for ages hoping someone else would let me in, and when they did I had to arrange to leave at the same time as him so's I could get out again. Still, I'm here now . . . what shall we do tomorrow, then?'

'It's so sunny that I thought I might go up on the moors,' Addy said. 'I take a sketch pad and find somewhere really beautiful and do the sketches, then usually I paint them at home. What did you want to talk about?'

'Well . . . you know the day you walked into the museum and nearly scared the life out of me?'

'Yes,' Addy said. 'Except I thought it was supposed to be you scaring the life out of me.'

He grinned. He had very nice teeth, white and even.

'That's what I wanted to tell you. Just before you appeared, I'd seen something very odd, or rather I thought I had.'

'Odder than me?'

The waitress bringing their coffees and dough-nuts had to dodge as Lance aimed a blow at Addy. They both subsided until she had left them again, then Lance shook his head sadly at her and continued.

'Honestly, no horseplay, now. Where was I? Oh yes, what I'd seen. Well, I'd been going round with Eva, who does guided tours, because she's leaving and they might want me to do the odd one from time to time – I told you before, didn't I? And part of Eva's routine is the old ghost business . . . you know, that some of the kids who died haunt the place.'

'Ghosts? When Betty said that I thought she was kidding,' Addy said, pricking up her ears. 'Are there really ghosts . . . I mean are there supposed to be ghosts, then?'

44

'Apparently. Eva said that there was one in the delft-room, that several people claimed to have seen her. She wears a brown coat and a longish skirt and she's got shoulder-length brown hair. They reckon it's the kid from the dipping-room who changed places with her little brother. Remember reading about it?'

'Yes, I remember. So, go on.'

'Well, there's a big mirror at the back of several of the displays, isn't there, to enable you to see the backs of the exhibits as well as the fronts.'

'Yes, I thought it was a great idea.'

'Sure. Well, I was looking into one of those mirrors and all of a sudden I saw what looked just like a girl . . . thin, with a browny coat and a greyish skirt on. She was coming towards me, she half raised her hand . . . I stepped back because it gave me quite a turn, I can tell you . . . and there you were!'

'Oh,' Addy said, rather disappointed. 'It was *me* in the mirror, then?'

'It must have been,' Lance said slowly. 'But afterwards, when I'd got over the scare it gave me, I wasn't so sure it was you. Only it must have been, of course.'

'Didn't you see her face?'

'Not really; the tilt of those mirrors is odd. I got a sort of double image from the glass, I suppose. I don't believe in ghosts, but I did wonder whether what I was seeing was something which had happened once, long ago, and somehow the image had hung around . . . Oh, I don't know, it sounds daft when you try to put it into words.'

'I think it's dead exciting,' Addy said, biting hugely into her doughnut. Her next words came out muffled. 'Dead exciting. We ought to have a proper ghost-hunt.'

'Oh, sure! With the place crowded with school parties, I suppose.'

'No, of course not. You've got keys, haven't you? Why don't we have a snoop round one evening, when it's getting dusk?'

Lance raised his eyebrows at her, all of a sudden mocking, making it seem that she was a credulous fool who had taken him seriously.

'Oh, yeah? Put my job on the line just to see a ghost who can't possibly exist? You have to be kidding!'

'We could pretend we'd left something in the museum and you'd let me in to find it,' Addy said obstinately, determined not to be put down by Lance's sudden air of superiority. After all, it had been he who had mentioned ghosts, not she! 'If I'm game, why should you be scared?'

'I'm not scared; it's just that I have keys to open up with, not to go night-snooping,' Lance pointed out. 'Anyway, do you believe in ghosts?'

'Not really,' Addy admitted. 'But I'm open-minded enough to admit I could be wrong. Aren't you?'

Lance stared down at the tablecloth, scowling, prodding at it with his cake fork. They had both eaten the enormously creamy doughnuts with their fingers despite the provision of forks. Addy watched the little holes appear in the cloth as Lance clearly considered her point.

'Tell you what. Suppose you and I take a picnic out on to the moors tomorrow? I'll pick you up at ten at your place, you can bung your sketching stuff into the car, and we'll make a day of it. Then

46

we'll talk about breaking and entering, because that's what they'd call it, I suppose.'

'That would be great,' Addy said. 'Let's meet somewhere, though. You don't want to trail all the way out to my place.'

'Yes, I do; it's easier. Give me your address and be ready at ten sharp because I hate hanging about.'

'I'm at forty-eight Carlton Street, but you won't know it,' Addy said reluctantly. 'You aren't local, are you? I mean you don't seem to know many people round here.'

'I was at school away,' Lance admitted, 'but I've lived just outside the town all my life. I know Carlton Street – as the crow flies it's not more than half a mile from the museum, is it? It's round the back, across the wasteland.'

'That's right,' Addy said. She was about to elaborate when Lance glanced at his wristwatch and jumped to his feet.

'Must go . . . got to get out at the same time as the guy who let me in,' he said briskly. 'Want a lift?'

But Addy was going shopping, so she refused, rather regretfully, and they parted with mutual promises to be on time next morning.

She had a lovely time buying some more clothes, then got fish and chips for dinner and cycled home fast so that they would still be hot by the time she got indoors. Her mother had said she'd be back for twelve-thirty. She felt great – she was going sketching next day and she loved drawing more than almost anything else – and Lance was taking her for a picnic and had bought her coffee and a doughnut, laughed with her, told

47

her about his ghost, a story she was sure he would only have told someone he trusted.

She was definitely on a high by the time she got home, longing to tell someone about her morning. She bounced into the kitchen with her new clothes in one hand and the newspaper-wrapped food in the other, dying to surprise Mum with a hot dinner and the story of her morning. But though she waited as long as she could, until the fish and chips were cold, her mother did not return.

Addy woke at seven next day, having decided to lie in, and got up at half-past. She was still sore with her mother, who had not reappeared all day, but the sun was shining and the birds were singing and it seemed silly to bear a grudge. So she padded downstairs in her old cotton pyjamas, fed Bunty, let her out, and then made tea and toast and carried it up to her mother's room.

'Come in,' Mum moaned at her third knock. Addy elbowed the door aside, only spilling a tiny puddle of tea, and clattered into the room. She put the tray down on the bedside table and went across and pulled back the curtains. Behind her, her mother groaned histrionically and reminded her cruel daughter that it was Sunday, but cheered up a bit when she saw the tea, the buttered toast and the jar of orange marmalade.

'Why breakfast in bed?' she asked presently, when her first cup of tea had been drunk and she was starting on the toast. 'It's not Mother's Day, is it?'

'No, of course not. It's just that I'm going out today, so I thought I'd make your breakfast for you. You were awfully late last night, weren't

48

you? I stayed up till midnight and you'd not come in then.'

'We went to a nightclub. I was with Stan, the feller I was telling you about – Stan Jackson. We had a grand time.' Mum's blonde hair looked tired in the fresh morning sun, her eyes bloodshot. She put a hand to her forehead and winced. 'Gawd, I've got a hangover; I shouldn't touch gin, if I've said it once I've said it a thousand times.'

'You never came in dinner-time, either,' Addy said. She had meant to sound joking but it came out reproachful. 'I'd got us fish and chips and ice-cream; Bunty and I had to eat the lot.'

'Well, you wanted independence, so I gave you some,' Mum said, sounding merely spiteful now. 'Spend all your money, did you?'

'I gave you half, like we agreed. I did spend the rest, though. I'll show you, presently.'

Mum drained her cup and poured another.

'All right, run along. Did you say you were going out today? I thought Di was working, Sundays. I went in to buy some fags and she said she was on all weekend.'

'Yes, but . . .' All of a sudden Addy did not want to explain about Lance and the picnic. Instead, she went to her room, calling over her shoulder, 'You'll get a surprise in a minute; don't get up till I come back.'

She put on the new jeans and the brightest, tightest T-shirt, then slung the denim jacket over one shoulder and put her feet into the light blue and white trainers she had bought. She would have liked to have had a go at her hair and tried a touch of the new make-up, but she knew her mother's concentration would not last long. If she

49

left her for more than two minutes, Mum would simply go back to sleep or get up. In neither event would she be a very satisfactory audience, so best get back quickly.

'Tan tara!' Addy said, posing in the door-way, chin up, hands low on hips. 'What do you think?'

Her mother stared, the cup of tea poised, motionless.

'Well, I'm damned! Who's this in aid of, then?'

'Me,' Addy said truthfully, because she would have bought the new things regardless of Lance. 'It's what other girls wear, Mum. Do I look nice?'

'You look . . . grown-up,' her mother said slowly. It sounded like a reproach. 'You'll start smoking next.'

'No, I shan't,' Addy said. She wished her mother could have said she looked nice, but at least she hadn't criticized. 'All I've done is buy a few clothes like all the other kids have. Nice, don't you think?'

Her mother unfroze and sipped tea, shaking her head.

'I suppose it had to happen sooner or later,' she said rather obscurely. 'Run along then; have a nice day.'

'Thanks,' Addy said. She went back to her room though and started properly this time, with a shower, a hairwash and lots of her new talc. As she was drying her hair with her mother's dryer she noticed that it wasn't such a dull brown after all; when the sun fell on it, it gleamed chestnut and gold, and it was shiny and silky, nice to touch.

Somehow this made her think of her mother's hair, which had lost all its shine and silkiness with the bleach and the perms, and vaguely, in her subconscious, something stirred. A something which could make sense of the childish, ugly clothes her mother had bought her and the way she seemed, sometimes, to be trying to push Addy back into the position of a dependent daughter, even to the point of wanting to take her wages. But it was pointless to think about it, especially on a sunny day when, very soon, Lance and his car would be at the door!

The car was a red sports model and had Addy opening her eyes very wide; it was most definitely not the sort of car you associated with a student working as general dogsbody and part-time guide at the Princeton Pottery Museum. Was it his dad's? Or an elder brother's? She knew almost nothing about him, she realized, but she would put that right with a whole day to do it in. But then the car drew up outside her gate and Addy rushed down the path, slammed the gate shut, and hurled herself into the passenger seat, her hair flying out behind her.

'No need to rush, we've got all day,' Lance said, revving the engine, but Addy, horribly aware of eyes watching her from number forty-eight, eyes which would laugh at her eagerness, think her freshly washed hair childish, undermine her new-found confidence, just laughed breathlessly and asked him, as they roared up the road, whether he could stop at a local shop so that she could buy some food.

'There wasn't much in the house,' she explained, trying to prevent her hair from wrapping itself round her face and gagging her. 'But I'll buy some sandwiches and a couple of Cokes if you stop somewhere.'

'No need,' Lance said, eyes front, hands on the steering wheel. 'I got my mother to make enough for two. If we're hungry at teatime though, you can buy us both chips and Coke then.'

'Lovely,' Addy said. She had captured most of her hair in one hand and was regretting being without the neat ponytail she wore for work, when Lance leaned forward and pulled something from the glove compartment. He handed it to Addy. It was a fine silk scarf, scarlet with a gold border.

'Thanks,' Addy said gratefully. She tied the scarf round her head and could not help noticing that it smelt beautifully of perfume. 'Whose is it?'

'My mother's. She hates getting her hair blown about so she leaves it in the glove compartment. Why do you ask?'

'Oh, I just wondered. I thought it might be your girlfriend's.'

He grinned, shooting a quick look at her.

'Don't have one. Too busy. At the start, too busy getting to college and then too busy staying there. In fact, this is the first summer I've felt I could have a bit of fun as well as working at a job and studying.'

'I see. What are you studying at college?'

'I'm doing a metallurgy degree. You know, maths, physics, stuff like that.'

Addy nodded silently; term after term, year after year, she had come bottom of her class in maths, physics and stuff like that.

'And what about you? Going to stick with the paint-room? Or do you want to move on into the modern factory later?'

'I'll have to stay where I am, I suppose,' Addy said a little dismally. 'It's fun in lots of ways and the money's lovely, but the work's dead boring – you wouldn't believe how boring it can be. Just painting poppies day after day, and no one seems to care if you get them right or wrong.'

'Well, from what the others say you can move into a better job if you want,' Lance contributed. 'I've heard on the grapevine that your pal Betty's going to be asked to do tour guides for the rest of the summer. She'll get a big pay increase and she'll meet lots of people, so perhaps you could try for that one day.'

'I'd hate it,' Addy said at once. 'I don't like talking to new people. No, what I want to do is to draw and paint, and that's why I said yes when Mum said there was a job going at the pottery. I thought they'd let me design . . . do freehand painting . . . that sort of thing. But it's just poppies, poppies, poppies!'

'Are you good enough to do freehand painting and design, though?' Lance asked, not being rude or anything, just wanting a straight answer. Addy could tell, because when he was getting at her his face had shown it and now his face was serious.

Accordingly, she did not take offence at what was a fair question.

'Yes, I think so,' she said. 'I've won lots of art competitions, got top grading last year, a year early, for the GCSE exam. The school wanted me to go to art college – assuming my other GCSE results are OK – but we have a bit of a struggle, Mum and me, so I started work instead.'

'And do you regret it?' Lance looked sideways at her, just a bit of a look. He was a good, steady driver, his hands resting lightly on the wheel, and he seldom took his eyes off the road for longer than a split second.

'No point,' Addy said briefly. She thought he might argue with this but he just nodded, then changed the subject.

'Anywhere special you want to go? If not, I . now a good place quite near here.'

'That will be fine,' Addy said politely. She hoped it was the sort of place she could sketch, but presently he turned off the road, at a point where the hills sloped gently up on one side of them and down on the other, bumping down a stony track which, as they went lower, even boasted a few scrawny, leaning trees.

'Nearly there – do you see that beck?'

It tumbled through its own rocky gorge, cut in the course of heaven knows how many years. It began high in the hills and fell and bounced recklessly down into the valley, where it promptly did a Jekyll and Hyde and became a bubbling, tinkling stream wending its way to the distant sea. On the flat, Addy guessed, it would meander over rocks and form quiet, deep pools, or find a level piece of ground and spread out into a miniature lake with sandy shores and reeds close to the water. But here it was still a beck, loudly announcing its presence as it crashed downwards.

'Yes, I see it. Can we eat by it, then?'

'We can. If you wouldn't mind opening the gate for me, when we reach it? You see, there's an abandoned miner's hut near here and the chap who owned it must have needed the track to get his ore to and from the main road. So I can drive down and leave the car by the hut, in the shade, too. Here we are.'

Addy jumped out, opened the gate and swung it closed when Lance had driven through. Then she climbed into her seat again.

'You know the country rules – always shut gates,' Lance said as she resettled herself. 'I was brought up in the country until I was twelve, so old habits die hard.'

'Oh? Why did you move into town, then?'

'Usual story. My father left, we couldn't afford the house, so we moved into the town. What about you?'

'Oh . . . well, my father went ages ago, before I was old enough to know anything, and my Mum and me lived with Gran for years – until she died two years ago, in fact. She was great, was Gran, she managed everything for all of us. I miss her more than you could imagine.'

'Yes. I miss my father. Not that he's gone right away. I mean, I see him; do you see yours?'

'No,' Addy said baldly. Once, she had been very curious about her father, but Gran had given her a talking-to and she had realized that Gran was right, it really didn't matter. Only . . . he had been artistic, Gran had let slip once, and she couldn't help wondering . . . she did not think he and her mother had actually married, though. Not that it mattered. Sometimes she wondered if

55

he even knew he had a daughter. If he knew, would he come back, move in with them, take care of Mum, who could do with someone to keep her on the straight and narrow? But it was just a wild sort of dream, really. Things like that didn't happen in real life – and possibly I'd hate him, resent being told what to do, Addy reminded herself. She did get cross, sometimes, when Mum tried to rule her life so why should a stranger who happened to have fathered her, years before, be any different?

'It was my father who gave me the car,' Lance said, having politely waited for Addy to expand on her monosyllable. 'He's great, Dad is – you'll like him.'

Addy shot him a quick, secret glance; was she going to meet him, then? But before she could ask, the car drew to a halt and Lance was getting out, coming round to her side of the car to open her door for her. He was very polite, she thought. Gran would have liked him very much . . . even her mother would appreciate the politeness.

'Well? What do you think?'

Addy just stood, drinking in the silence, the bees' song, the warmth of the sun. A heady perfume reached them from the short, wiry grass with its wild flowers and thyme, and when they got away from the car and walked towards the old stone-built building they could smell the sweet, nutty smell of the gorse blossom which grew closely against three sides of the tiny shed-like structure.

'It's beautiful,' Addy said. Her fingers itched to set it down on paper, capture the spare beauty of the stones, the tumbledown slate roof, the clustering gorse. 'Can we have our picnic by the water?'

The stream was a bright and noisy presence, and when they walked towards it they surprised a dipper, brilliant white throat and chestnut belly clear against the grey stone he was standing on, his little tail up, his eyes bright with surprise in the instant before he plunged like a salmon into the rushing water.

'I'll paint him when I get home,' Addy said comfortably, whilst they watched for him to reappear further up the stream. 'I do like dippers; they're so neat and tidy – it's the white throat, I suppose. It makes them look like wrens in dinner jackets.'

Lance laughed and set down a proper picnic basket on a convenient rock. Addy's previous picnics, even in Gran's day, had never included a basket and she was very impressed and said so, which made her companion laugh again.

'That's my mother for you – a very correct lady,' he said, opening the lid, and Addy got the impression just from his tone that for himself he would rather have had a little less correctness and perhaps a bit more scattiness. But it was an excellent picnic. Half a chicken each, which seemed needlessly generous, and lovely salads in Tupperware boxes with dressing and everything in little jars. Then beautiful dark brown bread crowded with grain, very interesting and crunchy to eat. Addy, brought up on sliced white, was really impressed with that bread.

'Butter in a little box . . . salt in a shaker . . . ooh, coleslaw, I love that,' she muttered as she withdrew all the interesting things and spread them out on the blue and white cloth Mrs Peterson had provided.

'Coldhamcoldbeefpickledgherkinssalad . . . ' chanted Lance rudely, quoting from *The Wind in the Willows*, and Addy threw the salt shaker at him and jeered when it caught him on the nose.

Lance, in revenge, picked her up and dangled her over the stream. Addy shrieked and hit out, Lance dropped her and slipped into the water as well and then they both climbed out, helpless with laughter, and lay on the bank in the sun to dry off.

'I haven't had such fun for years,' Lance said. 'Your face when you went in!'

'Yours was rather special, too,' Addy murmured. She sat up and reached for her sketch pad. Seconds later, Lance was staring at a picture of himself, mouth open, body starfishing, as he had plunged towards the water. He took it from her, examining it closely, then whistled.

'You're really good, woman! Gosh, you're wasted at the pottery. I reckon you might even be able to sell drawings this good locally. Why don't you ask at *Moorlands Crafts* if they'd be interested? It's probably just the sort of thing they'd love to be able to have on sale. Especially if you could do local scenes. And you want to get yourself into art college. Look, my mother's a single parent too but we manage.'

'Oh sure, but you're different, I expect,' Addy said lazily. She did not want to provoke an argument with Lance but it was clear as clear that the mother who had packed that picnic basket and the woman she had left in bed that morning were poles apart. There had been a strawberry shortcake for afters which Mrs Peterson had made

58

herself; Addy's mouth still watered at the recollection. Oh no, Mrs Peterson and Lila Bates would have nothing in common, she was sure of it.

'I grant you my father still supports her, but . . .'

'I'll think about it,' Addy promised. 'And I'm glad you like my drawing. As soon as I've had a snooze I'll go up and draw the miner's hut. I wonder why the miner left it?'

'Seam ran out, I imagine,' Lance said knowledgeably. 'It's padlocked now – did you notice? – but last time I came, a year or so ago with a friend, we got inside. We'd done something in school about the mining in these parts, so we searched and found his mine.'

'In the *hut*?' Addy said incredulously. 'Surely not.'

'Yes, actually in the hut. The miners dug from under cover, you see, so that when they left work they didn't have a slog through the rain or whatever to reach their home. It's very neat, just a square trapdoor in the floorboards with lino over it. I'd have liked you to see it . . . there's a fireplace, pretty rough though, and then you have a cupboard to one side of that and the trapdoor itself. We went down, of course. In this one you go about twenty metres, I should think, before it just comes to an end. Spooky, a bit, but rather exciting because you can't help wondering what would happen if the roof came in on you. Still, someone obviously decided it was dangerous, hence the padlock.'

'I'm going to take a look,' Addy said, intrigued by all this. 'Perhaps there's another way in, perhaps the padlock can be persuaded to open!'

She left Lance on the bank of the stream and made her way up to the hut. It was well-built, though there were gaping holes in the roof – she had seen that on the way down the hill – and the door was big and solid, not the sort of thing you could simply push at until it gave, as she had half hoped.

There was no window, which seemed odd, until she realized that the miner had probably kept the door open except in the evenings, when he would have needed artificial light anyway. However, the doorpost on one side had leaned and by applying her eye to the resulting crack she could just about see inside the hut.

She had expected it to be empty, but instead it seemed to be full of machinery – farming stock, she supposed vaguely. There were what looked like a couple of gas bottles, cylinders of some sort, on a trolley-like object. Clearly the farmer had left equipment here which he did not want stolen so he had bought himself a padlock.

Apart from the farm machinery, though, the hut seemed to be empty and because of the machinery she could not see the floor or the trapdoor or anything. Rather disappointed, she returned to Lance.

'I don't think it's padlocked because of the danger,' she said, flopping down beside him. 'Some farmer's left machinery in there.'

'Oh, then that explains it. Never mind, we'll come up again some time and see if we can get in if you're interested. And now I'm going to have a sleep, recharge my batteries.'

'Oh no you aren't. You can tell me about that ghost you thought you saw,' Addy said,

60

stretching and yawning in the sun. 'And we'll talk about our ghost-hunt.'

Lance groaned.

'Oh hell, I thought you'd forgotten all about it. I'm not going to risk my job and that's flat.'

'Scared?'

'No, of course not. I don't believe in ghosts. I'm just too keen to earn money, that's all.'

'I think you're scared,' Addy persisted. She did not think it for one moment but it was rather fun to needle Lance, she discovered.

'I'm not. But now we're talking about strange events, you can just repeat that conversation you overheard, as near word-perfectly as you can. And don't think I'm asking to be difficult because I do have a reason.'

'You do? Oh, all right.' Addy lay still for a moment, eyes shut, mind concentrating, then began to speak slowly, with much thought.

'First, a fellow with a local voice said something like "It's foolproof; if we get the heat right and Jacko can get transport we'll all be millionaires." '

'Good. And now the Scot.'

'Oh, yes. Right. He said, "There must be an awful lot, then." '

'Mm hmm, got that.' Lance, Addy saw, was writing busily on her sketch pad. Only on the cover she was glad to see since it was best paper and expensive. 'Go on.'

'Right. Then the local guy said, "It weighs heavy," and they'd been fetching it over for a while so it had added up. And then he said something about no one being fingered . . . not sure what that meant . . . and then that it was absolutely legal, that was the beauty of it.'

'Good. And then the Scot again?'

'No, it wasn't the Scot, it was Mr Braithwaite from Personnel. I recognized his voice at once. He said, "He's right, Ned. Once it's unmarked it's all absolutely legal and above board. Are you on?"'

'And then you switched off. Pity, but I don't blame you. Addy, I've given it a lot of thought and I believe you're on to something, though I'm damned if I know what!' He sighed, read his scribblings over to himself and then threw the sketch pad down. 'Oh well, I'll keep my eyes open and listen whenever the Scot, Ned, is around. He knows all about heat, doing the firing as he does, so I keep thinking that if only you'd heard a bit more . . . but never mind, it'll all be clear one day.'

'That's right.' Addy sat up and took her sketchbook. 'You think about it. I'm going to draw.'

She found a good spot to sit, with shade from a mountain ash and an uninterrupted view of the stone hut, then began to draw. But all the while, as she sketched, her mind was going round and round the possibility, the genuine possibility, that Lance had had a psychic experience and one, furthermore, which she might have as well, if only she could persuade him to go ghost-hunting with her one night.

She did not believe in ghosts, that was the odd part. And yet she had felt such tremendous sympathy for that child with her gap-toothed smile and straggly hair! Did ghosts put in an appearance because they wanted the living to do something for them, or was it just as Lance had said, that they were not there at all but you merely got a sort of moving picture show of what had once happened, from people who had been long gone but whose violent or tragic ends had somehow impressed themselves upon the very air?

Now that she had time to think about it, she was flattered that Lance had told her. Not many lads of eighteen or nineteen would admit to having thought they had seen a ghost, particularly to a girl of her age. Of course he'd kidded about it, claimed that it was her reflection in the glass . . . but could it have been so? She had been well down the room when Lance had appeared round the showcase. Could she possibly have been reflected from so far away?

And then something else occurred to her. She finished her sketch, made a note down the side of colours she was likely to need, and then returned to stand over Lance as he lay on the bank.

'Lance? Are you asleep? If so, wake up. I've had a thought.'

Lance sat up, yawned, then stumbled to his feet and went down to the water where they had put the bottle of cider to keep it cool. He fished it out, examined it through the glass and then announced with satisfaction that there was enough left for a mug each. Addy waited patiently whilst he filled the mugs, drank hers and then spoke whilst Lance was still wiping foam from his upper lip.

'Lance, when you saw the ghost, or whatever it was, you thought it was the ghost they talk about . . . the one with a brown jacket and a greyish skirt and shoulder-length hair, didn't you?'

'Only for a moment,' Lance protested defensively. 'I soon realized it couldn't be, of course, it must have been you.'

'Yes . . . only why?'

'Well, because you were there, for a start. And because you were wearing that brown blazer and your school skirt and you've got long hair.'

'And you saw my long hair? In the mirror, I mean?'

'Yes. All uncombed and straggly,' Lance said rudely. 'What next?'

'Nothing. Except that I had my hair tied back that day. I always have it tied back for work. So maybe it wasn't me you saw!'

4

They argued about it, on and off, all the way home. Lance said that he had been too startled to take in exactly what the girl had looked like, that she had probably had her hair pulled back just like Addy's . . . *must* have, since she was Addy. But Addy could see the doubt there, knew that he was puzzled by the whole experience and was intrigued by it, too.

According to plan they bought fish and chips and then Lance drove them to the common and parked so that they could eat them in peace and continue to talk.

Reluctantly, Addy had given in to Lance's insistence that they couldn't put their jobs on the line just to play around with a ghost-hunt, but she still thought that they might have a sighting during a dinner hour when the museum was shut to visitors but open to any member of staff who wanted to go round.

'The lights are off, the place is quiet . . . we must have a try, Lance!' she urged him. 'Come on, we won't be doing anything we shouldn't, you know we're welcome to visit the place whenever we want in our own time. Oh, and I never asked you – what were you doing that day, working when everyone else was on dinner hour?'

'I'd run out of money, so I thought I'd work then and go home early,' Lance admitted. 'My mother doesn't want me to take packed lunches, so usually I buy chips or a snack in the cafeteria upstairs, as you know.'

'I was hungry that day, too,' Addy admitted. 'I hadn't been paid and hadn't brought anything. Do you think we saw her because we were hungry?'

'You didn't see her,' Lance pointed out. 'And I wasn't hallucinating, if that's what you're trying to say.'

Addy nudged his chip paper crossly and a chip fell on to his jeans.

'No, of course it wasn't. I meant perhaps she showed herself to you from a sort of fellow-feeling . . . oh, I'm not sure I know what I *do* mean, now!'

'You're trying to steal my ghost,' Lance said blandly. 'Not content with your own mystery you're trying to muscle in on mine.'

'I'm sick of my mystery. I believe they're just making some different kind of china or porcelain or something which will make them all rich. That's all there is to it, I bet.'

'Oh, sure. Since when did china make a man a millionaire?'

'Yes, I can see what you mean,' Addy admitted grudgingly, after a pause for thought. 'All right then, both mysteries still stand. Lance, I think I ought to go home now, my mum's going to wonder what on earth I'm doing, getting back after she does.'

'Do her good,' Lance said lazily, but he screwed his chip paper into a ball and threw it on to the back seat. 'What'll she say when she finds out you've been kissing in a little red sports car?'

'I haven't,' Addy said, caught between amusement and embarrassment. 'Whatever makes you say things like that?'

Lance leaned over and put his arm round her. Then he pulled. Addy shot across the car, landing most uncomfortably on the brake, and found herself, for the first time in her life, being kissed.

She liked it. It was nice, warming . . . exciting even. Lance, however, appeared to be able to do it without breathing which was more than Addy, a mere beginner, could manage. Presently she pushed him away, took a deep breath, then leaned forward herself and gave him a tiny little kiss on the chin.

'Come on . . . take me home,' she commanded. 'We're back at work tomorrow!'

She had heard the girls at school talking about kissing and half wondered whether Lance would want to stay longer, kiss more, but he just grinned, rumpled her hair, and put the car in gear so that they bucketed off rather fast.

'Here we are,' Lance said, as they drew up quietly in Carlton Street. 'Safe and sound, just as Mum would want you. Enjoy yourself?'

'Yes, it's been tremendous, a really great day,' Addy said sincerely. She hoped he did not think she meant the kisses; she would have to think about that in the privacy of her own room. 'See you in the morning, Lance!'

She was a bit disappointed, in fact, that he had not tried to kiss her again, but went jauntily indoors, whistling softly beneath her breath. Though she had intimated to Lance that her mother would be home, she knew very well that it was most unlikely. She went quietly upstairs though, just in case, and was cleaning her teeth in the bathroom when she heard a voice calling her.

'Addy? Is that you? Oh, love, I do feel bad!'

Addy hurried into her mother's room. Her mother lay in bed, the light on, showing her face sickly white and drawn, her eyes set in pits of shadow.

'Mum! You're ill . . . what's happened?'

'Oh, Addy, I do feel dreadful; get the doctor, will you? There's a pain in my gut as though I'd got a wolf in there. Stan and me went out dancing and right in the middle of the tango I was took bad, so he brought me home. I thought all I needed was rest, but it's just got worse and worse. I'm really scared. Oh, I wish your Gran hadn't died!'

'I'll go next door,' Addy said worriedly. 'I'll wake them up if I have to; they'll let me use their phone.' She ran down the stairs, thinking sadly that she, too, often wished that Gran had not died. Gran had been such a tower of strength, always capable, seeing that Mum did the right thing, guiding their small family through the mysteries of rent tribunals, the health service and even Pay As You Earn, which had baffled Mum for years and always led to indignant outcries whenever she got a pay cheque.

But now Gran was gone, and all unwilling, Addy seemed to have stepped into her shoes.

After all, if Mum had been feeling ill for hours, surely she could have staggered round to the neighbours? Still. Addy thundered down the stairs and out of the house, dashed down the garden path and up next door's. She hammered on their polished oak with its eye-level stained glass – they had bought the house; she and Mum were still tenants – and then, for good measure, rang the bell hard.

Mr Evans, small, weasel-faced, suspicious, came to the door in pyjamas and slippers, but he could not have been kinder once she told him what had happened. He woke Mrs Evans, who made tea and then went straight round to comfort Mrs Bates whilst Addy rang the doctor, got his wife, got an emergency number, could not understand what the hospital doctor the other end was saying, and finally ran to earth someone who said they would be round with an ambulance in less than twenty minutes.

In fact, it was thirty, and then there was a good deal of toing and froing before the doctor announced that Mrs Bates seemed to have a ruptured appendix and would go straight to the Princeton General for an emergency operation.

'I'll come,' Addy insisted, and got in the ambulance despite the doctor, who hovered around assuring her that there would be nothing she could do for her mother once they arrived, that she would only be in the way.

'Come, Addy,' her mother moaned. 'Do come with me . . . I'm that scared!'

Addy stayed until her mother, only semi-conscious now, was wheeled into the operating theatre and then she gave in, having been told that she could ring the hospital for a progress report first thing, but that she would not be allowed to visit for at least twelve hours.

The taxi took her right to the door and the driver insisted on watching her in, then drove away with a toot on his horn which probably woke the half of the neighbourhood which had managed to sleep through Addy's carelessly loud closing of the front door.

She prowled through the house at first, convinced that she was far too worried and tired to sleep, but Bunty was curled up in an armchair, the house seemed tidy enough, and so she went and got into bed, telling herself that she should count sheep, or poppy mugs, to give herself at least a chance of some rest.

In fact, she scarcely remembered her head touching the pillow, but slept like the dead until morning.

'She's come round, but now she's asleep again,' the sister on the ward told Addy when she rang at nine o'clock, just about as soon as she had woken. 'You may come for half an hour this evening, but come to my office first. We've got to keep your mother quiet for a day or two.'

Addy went into work late, explained to Beryl and was promptly sent off to the cafeteria to get herself some breakfast. Instead of eating at once, however, she prowled round until she found Lance, polishing showcases in the Korean-room and whistling happily.

He was very concerned about her mother's condition and promised to take her to visit the hospital that evening and then to have tea at his home. To stop her having to worry about food, as he put it. Addy was not too sure that having tea with a stranger – Lance's mother – would be very relaxing, but she agreed to go simply because she dreaded being alone. Poor Mum, all pale and wan in a hospital bed . . . Gran would have bustled in with all sorts of comforts. Addy spent her time in the cafeteria eating buttered toast and drinking tea, but also making a list of necessities which her mother should be given. And when she got back to the paint-room, feeling a good deal more human, she realized that she should have got in touch with her mother's people at work to tell them why she would not be in for a while.

Beryl, however, had thought of it all.

'I phoned through and your mum's friend Freda says she'll see to things. Don't worry, now they know she's in hospital they'll make sure she gets sick pay and so on.'

To do her credit, Addy had not even given money a thought but now that she had, it was nice to know that they would not be penniless until her mother could work again – apart from her own money, of course, but that really did shrink to size when you considered having to pay the rent and so on with it.

'Thanks, Beryl,' she said with real gratitude. 'I wouldn't have known what to do. It's very kind of you. By the way, where's Betty?'

'Oh, love, what a bad moment to have to lose your pal!' Beryl's brown eyes softened, showing she really was sorry. 'Not but what it's good for Betty – she's guiding for the rest of the summer, she won't be working in here any more.'

Addy sighed but said she was glad for Betty and returned to her bench, grabbing the next mug and painting poppies with vengeful speed. So Betty would be guiding today, with Eva! Which meant she would be in the museum instead of the workrooms, except when she was guiding parties round, of course. Addy was surprised by the sharp surge of resentment which filled her at the thought of Lance and Betty working together. Lance would obviously fall for Betty – she was so pretty and such good fun.

By dinner-time she was feeling definitely anti-Lance, which was both silly and unfair, but that made no difference. She walked over to the museum and opened the white glazed door which was the staff way into the foyer, more than half expecting to see Lance and Betty locked in a passionate embrace against the counter, so violently had her imagination been at work. But instead there was Lance, on the telephone, with his long back bent to get his head inside that little plastic hood thing, looking somehow like a heron in a hairdryer. This made Addy laugh and she was still smiling when Lance emerged and shook himself, straightening. He smiled at Addy.

'Phew, those things weren't built for normal-sized people, only for little dwarfs, like you! My mother's really pleased I'm bringing you home for tea and says can she get anything for your mother, and do you like raspberries, so I said everyone does. I mean I've never seen you turn your nose up at anything, so far as I can recall.'

'Are you calling me greedy?' Addy said indignantly. She had meant the question to be rhetorical, but Lance insisted on answering it with a 'Yes!' so that she cuffed him and they exchanged a few half-hearted insults before Lance suddenly remembered that she would want to ring the hospital again and got out a handful of ten-pence pieces.

He really was thoughtful, there was no doubt about it. Addy only needed one coin though, because the sister said that Mrs Lila Bates was doing nicely and that seemed to end the conversation. But, 'Tell her I rang; tell her I'll be in to see her straight after work,' Addy insisted, knowing that her mother would be needing all the moral support she could get. Sister had already warned her that Mum had been in intensive care – was still there, in fact – but would be moved to a side ward later in the day. Side wards were single rooms, Sister said so, and Addy knew all about intensive care. Mum would be scared out of her wits half the time and bored silly the other half. She had no reserves in her mind for solitude, Addy knew. Mum needed other people, soap operas on telly, admiring men-friends, then she'd be fine, but left to her own devices she would just pine.

Still, Sister said comfortingly that she would pass on the messages, and then Addy rang off and turned at once to Lance, who was hovering beside her.

'I've got to go shopping,' she explained quickly. 'Mum's going to need all sorts. The trouble is, I went and spent all my money over the weekend . . . I suppose . . . '

'Want me to lend you some dosh?' Even before Addy had got to the stammering, red-faced bit, Lance was diving into his jeans' pocket. 'Twenty quid? More?'

'A tenner would be fine,' Addy said. 'I'll pay you back Friday, soon's I get my money, straight up.'

"Course you would, but you hang in there until your mother's out of hospital and sorting you out,' Lance said robustly. 'Come on, take the twenty, you'll be astonished how fast it goes.'

She was. Two really light women's magazines made a hole in a fiver; Mum's favourite talc was over two quid; oranges, grapes and paper hankies in a fancy box with a packet of cologne wipes free with each purchase pretty well saw off the first ten.

'I'll buy her chocolates,' Lance said when he saw Addy hovering over an impossibly expensive box of her mother's favourites. 'Don't forget she'll be in for several days yet, and you'll be wanting to take her something each evening, I dare say.'

Addy looked at him with some awe. She put the chocolates back on the shelf and, after some thought, put the talcum powder back as well. For a mere man he was very far-seeing, she considered. But she bought a smaller box of chocolates, though she felt guilty doing it with his own money.

'For your mother, for asking me to tea,' she explained, and Lance was pleased, she could tell. What was more, he took advice as well as handing it out, because when she put some of her things back he said might he give Mrs Bates the talcum and she graciously allowed him to do so.

'And my mother told me to buy a bottle of Lucozade, from her,' Lance said, which seemed a bit over the top to Addy, but she knew her Mum would be pleased. Little things like that were nice, when you weren't well. Addy rounded off her purchases with the most showy 'get well' card on the shelves and then the pair of them had to run all the way back to the museum or they would have been late for work.

'Well? How is she?'

Lance was standing in the hospital foyer waiting for Addy and fell into step beside her as she headed for the exit. He had given her the talcum and Lucozade with a card, but had refused to go along even to the swing doors at the end of the ward, sure that Addy's mum would not want to see a stranger at a time like this.

He had been right; Addy's mother, pale and listless, with her hair duller and her body more shapeless than Addy had ever seen them, had absolutely no desire to see a strange young man.

'Hello, love,' Mum said, kissing Addy and clutching her hard for a moment. 'What you got there? Oh, thank goodness, me own nightie, and some scented soap . . . the sister said you'd bring 'em. What's the rest?'

'A few presents,' Addy said, putting the paper bags down on the counterpane. 'You aren't to worry about anything, your friend Freda's managing the work side, everyone's been very kind, and my friend Lance and his mother sent you some bits and bobs . . . and there's cards.'

Addy's mother brightened visibly as she began to open the parcels, but Addy was a bit dismayed to see that her mum was still on a drip, with tubes leading out of her arm and sinister-looking bottles on a stand by the bed.

'Ooh, lovely!' her mother kept exclaiming. She looked up. 'What about Stan, then, in Despatch? I don't want him thinking I've stood him up; that's not my way.'

Her voice was small and hoarse; she sounded as different as she looked, Addy thought.

'I think Freda will tell him, but I'll make sure tomorrow,' Addy promised. 'Can he visit you . . . I mean do you want him to?'

'Not yet,' Mum said hurriedly. 'Not till I'm more meself. I'll want a bit of make-up first. Now, how about you, Addy? Are you all right, love? Managing without me?'

'I miss you awfully,' Addy confessed, knowing she was speaking the truth. Annoying though her mother was at times, she still missed her company, even though they were often like ships in the night, passing each other in the kitchen or living-room as they got ready for work or, in her mother's case, went out on the town.

Mrs Bates smiled palely.

'I'm glad you miss me, but I miss you much worse,' she confessed. 'I miss the house, and Bunty, and me own bed. I'm desperate to come home.'

'You come when they say you can,' Addy said. 'Mum, Lance is outside, the lad I told you about from work. He brought me in his car and he's going to take me home again. Want me to fetch him in to say hello?'

Her mother's incorrigible eyes had brightened at the mention of a male, then they dulled again. She was clearly still far from her normal self.

'No, love, not whilst I feel so poorly,' she said. 'And I smell of hospitals and operations, too.'

'You smell fine, but I won't bring him in,' Addy said. She got out the cologne wipes and used one on her mother's pale forehead, then smoothed it down on to her hands and wrists. Mum closed her eyes and a little smile played about her dry lips.

'Nice,' she murmured. 'You're a good girl, Addy. Did I mention that I like them jeans and things you bought? They suited you.'

Addy smiled, but before she could say anything she realized that her mother had fallen asleep, and after stroking her brow gently with the cologne wipe for a few minutes she stole very quietly out of the side ward and on to the main ward itself, where she found Sister helping a nurse to change someone's bed.

'She's sleeping,' Addy said when Sister asked her how her mother seemed. 'Will she be in that little room long, Sister? Only my mum's better off with people round her. She'll be happier on the main ward with everyone else.'

Sister nodded but said that for the time being Doctor wanted Mrs Bates kept quiet, and Addy was forced to admit that if her mother could fall asleep at six in the evening then she really did need her rest.

'She'll be fine in a day or so,' Lance said consolingly as he held the car door open for her and slammed it behind her. The roof was still down and the sun still shone brightly. 'Just give her time,' he added as he walked round to the driver's door. 'These parents can be quite a worry to sons and daughters.'

He little knew how right he was, Addy thought ruefully, as they left the town centre behind and began to drive through leafy suburbs. But Mum was all right, really; when she'd said that about the jeans looking nice, Addy had recognized – and accepted – the apology which she knew was intended, even though her mother hadn't actually used the word.

'Here we are,' Lance said at last. He slowed the car, indicated right and slid into a tree-lined drive. 'You'll not worry about my mother if she's . . . well, if she goes on a bit, will you?'

Addy snorted with laughter.

'Like you do, d'you mean? It won't worry me!'

Lance aimed a cuff at her but she ducked, and then the car was slowing and stopping before a small Georgian house built of grey stone with cream-painted shutters and a heavy oak front door, and before it a circular lawn, a fountain in a fish-pond, and several colourful flowerbeds.

'And this is what you came down to, after you moved from the country?' Addy gasped, getting slowly out of the car and on to the beautifully raked gravel. 'Christ!'

'It's a bit more complicated than that,' Lance muttered. He fussed round the car, clearly wanting a moment to themselves before they entered the house. 'My father bought it for us, as a business proposition really. We take care of it and have the nicest flat, the right-hand ground-floor one. And we do the garden, or most of it. The rest gets done either by keen tenants, if we have any, or by a chap who comes in two afternoons a week. Do you like it?'

'Yes,' Addy breathed. Behind the house she could see more garden, tall trees, a huge lawn.

'Well, you wouldn't if you had to rake the bloody gravel and mow the lawns and weed the flowerbeds,' Lance said bitterly, beneath his breath. 'Nor if you had to paint the shutters and balance on stepladders to reach a ceiling miles high, with moulded fruit and flowers which take hours to emulsion. When I'm earning I'm going to have a tiny little flat in a huge big block where someone else does everything!'

'Oh well, it's good training for you,' Addy said, as they moved over the gravel towards the front door, climbing a flight of spotless white stone steps to do so. 'You could take a job as a butler any day, I reckon.'

Lance laughed and opened the front door. He ushered her into a wide hall and then produced a key and opened the large right-hand door.

'Sure I could! Here we are, then. Angela!'

Addy hoped that Angela would not turn out to be a maid in a black uniform and frilly apron, but instead a tall woman with a big bosom and a tiny waist emerged into the hall. She had one hand extended and a smile of welcome on her lips and Addy knew at once that this must be Mrs Peterson. She had large, light blue eyes with lids which drooped as though almost unable to bear their own weight, a soft, rather querulous mouth which looked as though it sighed a lot, and very white skin. Her hair was fair and cut into a pageboy which curled under beautifully, her nail polish was a lovely cinnamon-brown shade, and she wore a biscuit-coloured linen dress which showed off her excellent figure, and earth-brown shoes with the highest heels Addy had ever seen.

'Angela, this is Addy Bates. Addy, my mother.'

Mrs Peterson murmured that it was lovely to meet her boy's friend at last and swooped, scentedly kissing Addy's unprepared cheek, then stood back and received the chocolates which Addy was clutching with what appeared to be genuine and unfeigned pleasure.

'Darling . . . Lance must have told you these were my favourites,' she exclaimed. 'Well now, dear, and how is your mother? Feeling a little better, I trust?'

Addy, rather overawed, replied that her mother was indeed better, though still far from herself, and watched as Mrs Peterson drifted about the room, straightening a rug, moving a picture a little to the right or left and chatting in her slow, cultured voice. The room was lovely, too. The furniture was all old – antique, Addy supposed – but beautiful, the wood glowing with age and polish, the chintz which covered the easy chairs faded to soft pinks, creams and fawns. The window overlooked the front garden and was open at top and bottom so that the scents from the roses which grew nearby could be enjoyed by those within the room, and the carpet was just a square of more soft, faded colours, sitting on a sea of gleaming golden parquet flooring. There were pictures, just three, and they all had that indefinable air of quality which told Addy that they were not just daubs but beautiful original oil paintings of places which, perhaps, Mrs Peterson had once known and loved.

'Well, now that we've met, we'd better have our tea, or you two children will be too tired for work tomorrow,' Mrs Peterson said at last, having indulged in a very one-sided conversation with Lance about people Addy had never heard of. Lance had looked embarrassed all through the conversation, whilst Mrs Peterson had talked about 'Dear Sir Henry, that lovely old lady down by the mill, and the person in the shop on the corner who persists in calling me Miss Angela, as though I hadn't been married for more years than I care to mention.'

Now, she led the way back into the small hall – cream and gold striped paper, more polished flooring and two pictures in gilded frames – and through into another room. It was clearly a dining-room, with a long table polished to mirror-like brilliance, a great big looking-glass with cherubs and grapes in gilt around it, and four old, old chairs with ornately carved backs and slippery leather seats.

But Addy only gave the room the most cursory of glances and then concentrated on staring at the food. There was a crusty pork pie, plates spread with sliced chicken, ham and beef, several different sorts of salad, jacket potatoes wrapped in foil to keep them hot and, at the far end of the table, a chocolate gateau, a trifle with cream on the top and, best of all, raspberry meringues!

'Sit down,' Mrs Peterson said hospitably. 'Now just help yourself, Addy, don't be shy. I want to see all this food eaten, because that's what food is for, isn't it?'

There's no answer to that, Addy thought, nevertheless politely agreeing and seeing, with amusement, a brief look of anguish flash across Lance's face. Mothers, she decided, whether they

81

call themselves Mum or Angela, do say some daft things at times!

'I love to cook; it's a relic of my past, I dare say,' Mrs Peterson remarked, as they passed around the pork pie. 'I expect Lance has told you that I was on the stage for years? Well, on the stage you keep moving on from town to town, or you did then, and of course you never had time to cook and were very much at the mercy of landladies, or hotels. So cooking, for me, became not a chore but a pleasant recreation, and once my fellow Thespians discovered I was good at it, they were quite willing to pay for ingredients and persuade me to cook for them. And I, of course, was equally willing to indulge in my favourite pastime. And now, as Lance may have told you, I cook commercially.'

'Oh? Do you work for a canteen or something?' Addy said unwarily, and surprised a very sharp look from those large blue eyes. Mrs Peterson, however, gave a little trill of laughter and leaned across the table to tap Lance playfully on the hand.

'Oh, Addy, I can see my boy doesn't exactly chatter about his home life whilst he's at work! No, indeed, but I make wedding cakes and special-occasion cakes, and I sometimes do a dinner party for someone if it's the sort of thing which appeals to me. Since I was left to bring Lance up alone I've had to work, to let the rest of the house and so on. But we get along, don't we, dear?'

Lance, eating very fast, said that they did.

'I don't cook, or only things like potatoes, and I don't like housework very much,' Addy

82

confessed. 'It's a good thing our house is small.'

'Well, Lance can be quite a help,' Mrs Peterson said. 'He doesn't like gardening – I love it – but he'll do the rough work, digging, mowing lawns and so on. He's even done some decorating, haven't you, dear?'

'Masses,' Lance said gloomily. He looked meaningfully up at the ceiling and Addy, following his eyes, saw the plaster flowers and fruit he had complained about. 'There isn't a ceiling in this entire house that I haven't painted at some time or another.'

'Oh, ceilings!' Mrs Peterson dismissed ceilings with a flicker of long, red-tipped fingers. 'The trouble is, I like things nice and so it does seem that as soon as we finish one job another appears. I'm afraid we single parents do rather *rely* on our children, Addy – no doubt your mother is the same – but Lance never lets me down.'

'How do you manage when he's away at college?' Addy asked. She had noticed that Lance called it college and not university.

It was the wrong thing to say. Lance took a mouthful of food and she could see he was trying not to grin, but Mrs Peterson sighed deeply and shook her head.

'How indeed? I *begged* him, Addy, not to leave me here to manage alone. A woman in a house this size needs a man, just to keep it running smoothly, but he would go. He went on and on about his future – as if I didn't understand perfectly that he needed a degree – but I'm sure he could have studied at the Tech and done every bit as well. It would have meant he came home at night, you see. And then, to add insult to injury,

83

he went out and got himself this job, so even in the long vac, when I'd planned all sorts of things, I had to fit all the jobs into weekends or evenings.'

'Well, we all need some money, even students,' Addy said in what she hoped was an understanding tone. Poor Lance! Mum's faults were shrinking with every word Mrs Peterson uttered!

'Oh, money! It's that car – his father gave it to him, but he didn't think to increase his allowance. Oh no, he just gave him a great big added expense, that's all, with never a thought for me. I can't give my boy a car, or . . .'

'Angela, don't forget Mr Gillman. Where would you be without him? You said it at least . . . you said it yesterday. You told him how marvellous he was when he was piling the lawn clippings into black bags for me to drive down to the tip. Don't forget your favourite tenant!'

Mrs Peterson lowered her head and then looked up at Addy through her long, beautifully darkened lashes. She gave a little, dreamy smile. *Was* an actress? She still is, and a hammy one at that, Addy thought unkindly as Mrs Peterson mimed coyness, you've-discovered-my-secret and other ridiculously overstated emotions. Honestly!

'Oh . . . Brian Gillman, you mean.' Mrs Peterson turned to Addy, the coy look still very much in evidence. 'He's marvellous, my dear – adores me, can't do enough – but I'm afraid of getting too involved, too dependent. After all, I don't want to marry again – once bitten, twice shy – and I don't want Brian to feel I'm leading him on.'

'He won't; he's a nice chap,' Lance said in heartening tones, but Mrs Peterson shook her head at him, making her hair swing forward.

'I often wonder if there's a touch of jealousy there,' she said ruminatively. 'The pair of you hovering round the lawnmower . . . but who's to say?' She turned to Addy, suddenly brisk. 'Finished, dear? Then how about a slice of my chocolate gateau? Or some cream and sherry trifle?'

At the end of the meal Mrs Peterson proposed that Lance should wash and wipe up whilst she and Addy had a nice chat, but this Addy would not stand for. Gently but firmly she went into the beautiful, modern little kitchen which overlooked the spread of lawn, put on the red rubber gloves which, she assumed, guarded Angela's hands when Lance was in college and unable to do the dishes, and washed up whilst Lance wiped and put away.

Mrs Peterson, foiled of her prey, followed them into the kitchen and perched on a kitchen stool, cleaning off what looked to Addy like perfectly good nail polish and applying another layer, waving her hands languidly like a cormorant drying its wings after a plunge. Then she applied a specially rich sort of handcream, she told Addy, since housewives' hands need extra care.

'A woman has to make sure she looks her best all the time,' she told Addy impressively, as the two younger people worked. 'Men think women are nothing but household slaves once they've got you tied to the home with children and so on. Men like that, a woman at their beck and call, but it isn't the hardworking housewives they run off with when they're bored, oh, no! It's the pretty young things with nothing to do but enjoy themselves and chase men, that's who they run off with. Why, when Lance's father left me it was suggested that I should go out and get a job, try to keep myself and the boy! Why should I do that, I thought, when my husband has simply run away from us and his responsibilities? So I'm afraid Lance's father didn't escape from domesticity quite as cleverly as he thought he would; he pays quite a lot of my bills, helps towards Lance's college expenses, and has to keep That Woman into the bargain.'

'Dad did offer to help run the car, Angela,' Lance said, his tone carefully neutral. 'That's why I work . . . one of the reasons. And I pay for my keep here.'

'Lance, dear, you're very good, very good indeed, but don't run away with the idea that what you pay me goes very far,' Mrs Peterson said. 'Now I can see you've done – did you put the silver away? I hope in the right drawer, there's nothing worse than going to the knife drawer and finding a fork, don't you agree, Addy?'

'I'm afraid I'm not awfully fussy about things like that, Mrs Peterson,' Addy confessed. 'But I'm tidy with my work-things, which is probably the same.'

Free of the house, having said her thanks and farewells, Addy told Lance that she was impressed that anyone could keep knives and forks separated, let alone in different drawers.

'Ours are all bundled into a tatty little wooden box under the sink,' she told Lance as she climbed into the car. 'Your mother is . . . is remarkable, really she is, Lance.'

'She drives me *mad*,' Lance said through gritted teeth. 'She promised . . . if I'd bring a friend home she wouldn't go on about Dad or Ginette – that's his new wife – or moan to you that I'm selfish to go to college. And what does she do? She moans about me and goes on about Dad! Bloody woman!'

'She's all right really,' Addy said tolerantly. 'It's a lovely house and that was a super tea. You're lucky she can cook like that. My mum burns water and once I *carved* her rice pudding!'

Lance smiled, but you could see it was reluctantly. He started the car and slammed it into gear, then drove off too fast, spurting gravel. It looked deliberate but Addy realized his mind was miles away and anyway, since he cut the grass he would suffer personally for that scattered gravel.

'Look, Addy, we might as well get this straight. My mother tells lies about Dad and Ginette. Ginette's only a couple of years younger than Angela, for a start, not exactly a 'pretty young thing', and she doesn't need Dad to keep her, she's chief designer for a big garment manufacturing firm. She loves Dad, she doesn't just see him as a meal ticket, and that's what he'd become to Angela, however she may try to wrap it up.'

'I don't understand about husbands and wives,' Addy said honestly, after a pause. 'But your mother's very kind . . . and pretty, too. I suppose she was hurt that your father liked someone else better.'

'Yes. She was. I shouldn't say things about her, you never moan about your mother, but Angela's awfully wearing to live with, really she is. Everything's got to be perfect and that fellow, Brian Gillman, gets shoved down my throat sometimes till I could go up and wring his neck.'

'But he helps,' Addy pointed out. 'You said he helped.'

'Oh, he does. He and Angela have got some fiddle going . . . it's something to do with what Dad pays her – I'm not sure about it – which means he pays less rent than the others in the house but makes up for it by gardening, taking Angela shopping when I'm not there to do it and so on.'

'He sounds a gem to me,' Addy said. 'Don't grumble, just pray he asks your mum to marry him.'

Lance grinned, then slowed the car; they had reached Carlton Street.

'All right, I get the message. So what's your mother like, then? Small and neat and cheerful, like you?'

Addy laughed at this description of herself. It was funny to think that Lance had never met Lila Bates.

'Like me? Not a bit. She's a bottle-blonde, hates housework, can't cook, won't garden, loves going out and having a gay old time, spends all her money on clothes, make-up and fags . . . but she could be worse. I'm fond of her except when she makes me so mad I could scream, and she's fond of me most of the time. But she doesn't like having a daughter of my age because it makes her see she's getting on a bit, I suppose.'

'Well, I'm darned,' Lance said, turning off the engine as the car slid to a halt outside number forty-eight. 'Look, I'm guiding a tour with Betty tomorrow afternoon, so I'll be mugging up my stuff in the dinner hour, but I'll meet you in the courtyard at half-five, and I thought we might go to the cinema after you've seen your mum.'

'Guiding a tour? With Betty? Why? I thought she was working with Eva.'

Addy's hackles were up; she should have guessed that once Betty was working in the museum Lance would realize how very pretty and bright the older girl was! No wonder he had only kissed her once . . . he might just as well take Betty to the cinema if he wanted to go. She, Addy, had better things to do with her time.

'She does work with Eva but we've got two school parties booked in at the same time, and so the boss said Betty and I could take one and Eva the other. She's good already though, Betty is. I was really impressed this morning.'

'Oh? Did you go with her this morning, too?'

The remark came out not casually, as Addy had intended, but sharply, with bite. Lance looked surprised.

'No, of course not. But I was in the Korean-room, sweeping through, when she brought a party in. And she was as slick as though she'd been guiding for a year, I thought.'

'Oh,' Addy said, the wind taken out of her sails by this forthright explanation.

'OK then – I'll see you in the courtyard, five-thirty.'

She was half out of the car this time before Lance leaned across and pulled her back.

'Far be it from me to demand payment for Angela's cooking, but . . .'

89

Kissing, Addy decided five minutes later, wobbling unsteadily up her front path, improved with practice. And somehow, she no longer worried about Betty and the guided tours. Kissing also, it seemed, put things into perspective!

5

It was dull in the paint-room next day without Betty, and duller having solitary sandwiches without Lance, but pride kept Addy well away from the museum. She accepted that Lance was really working with Betty and did not fancy her, or not as much as he seemed to be fancying Addy herself, at any rate. But she did not want it to appear that she was following them around. So she went and sat on a pile of bricks in the long grass near the old disused kiln, and ate her sandwiches in solitary state and thought.

She was missing her mother in the mornings, but it was definitely easier with only one person wanting the bathroom, and with no one to interfere with her sandwich-making. Mrs Bates never took a packed lunch but she saw no reason why Addy should, either, so didn't bother to buy in the necessary ingredients. Addy, doing her own marketing in her dinner hour, with Lance along sometimes, bought things which didn't need too much work – sliced bread, sliced ham, tomatoes and apples, things like that. What was more, she had toast and tea for breakfast without having to bawl up to her mother every five minutes that if she didn't hurry she wouldn't get fed. Mum didn't *mind* not getting fed, but Addy remembered Gran's strictures about leaving the house with an empty stomach and always tried to see that her mother had something, if only a cup of tea and one round of toast.

She had rung the hospital first thing this morning, as she made a habit of doing, and the Sister said that Mrs Bates might be home in a day or so, and she had felt a real lift of the heart at the thought. I'm not frightened of being alone in the house, Addy told herself defensively now, but it was impossible not to imagine things. Every board that creaked might have been an intruder, and though you could tell yourself a million times a minute that no intruder with a grain of brain would break into a house like theirs, Addy's internal worrying clock still clicked into action with each tiny night-sound.

But now, in the sun, eating ham and radish sandwiches and thinking about going to the cinema with Lance, Addy was at the dreamy, delicious stage when something tore past her through the grass, giving a fearful yowl as it did so. Addy began to get to her feet – and was promptly knocked off them again by a small but heavy dog, a bull-terrier, all grin and slanting eyes, which was pursuing the yowler so singlemindedly that it had not even noticed Addy until it hit her behind the knees.

Addy staggered upright again and saw the yowler. It was poor Bunty, going like the wind it was true, but fat and frightened and desperate, not at all her usual smug self.

'Hey . . . come here, you dog!' Addy shouted, but wasted no more breath in words. She set off in pursuit and was going at her fastest when the old disused kiln loomed up ahead of her.

The bull-terrier was going too fast to stop, too fast to corner properly either. He slid on his side and Addy fell on top of him, whumping all the breath out of his body and considerably startling the man who had been halfway out of the old kiln as they shot past.

Addy had scarcely seen him save for a white, frightened face with the dark 'o' of his mouth gaping with astonishment, and then he had retreated back into the old kiln and shut the door.

But not before Addy had caught a glimpse of a big block of something-or-other behind him. And machinery.

However, she had no time to wonder, not with a muscular and fast-recovering bull-terrier beneath her and Bunty, clearly out of breath and believing herself to be safe, slowly plodding across the grass towards the courtyard.

'Run, Bunty!' Addy shrieked, and grabbed the bull-terrier's collar.

Someone must have heard the shrieks and the snortings as the bull-terrier tried to get out from under Addy and to free itself from her grip on its collar. One of the girls from the paint-room shouted, another plucked the trembling Bunty out of the grass, and Addy rolled off the terrier, which promptly shook itself free and sat back, panting, with a yard of pink tongue hanging out and its small, Chinese eyes trying to assure her that it had meant no harm, that some of its best friends were cats.

'Oh, all right,' Addy said grudgingly, seeing that Bunty was safe. 'But you shouldn't be here at all, and nor should Bunty. Oh dear, now what do I do?'

She dared not let the bull-terrier roam free there, though. The breed had a reputation, probably undeserved, for fierceness, but even if it was as mild as milk it still could not be allowed to wander the museum grounds, not with two school parties due shortly.

Her dilemma was solved for her as she crossed the courtyard, the dog trotting docilely at her side. The fact that she had a hand still on his collar meant that she had to walk bent over, so that she almost missed seeing Lance.

'Hello!' came his amused voice from somewhere above her head. 'What's all this, then? Taken a prisoner?'

Addy looked up and there, leaning out of the office window, was Lance, grinning.

'Oh, hello,' Addy said sheepishly. 'I've caught this dog trying to make mincemeat out of my cat, Bunty. I didn't think it ought to be roaming about here loose, and I've no idea how it got in. I suppose Bunty must have climbed the wall, but this chap couldn't possibly have done anything so athletic.'

'Bunty?'

'He was chasing her,' Addy admitted. 'But I collared him before any harm was done. What on earth do I do now, though?'

'Oh, it's all right, he's probably escaped from Ned Armstrong's car,' Betty said, appearing suddenly beside Lance. 'Aren't you brave, Addy? He's a guard dog, you know, horribly fierce.

94

Ned lets him roam free if he's working late here, nights.'

I don't think he knows he's horribly fierce, or only when he sees a cat,' Addy said, continuing to cling to the dog's collar. 'Can you get hold of Ned Whatshisname, d'you think? I dare not let him go, he's an awfully fast runner despite his size.'

'I'll give him a tinkle,' Betty shouted, whilst Lance continued to grin down into the courtyard. 'Just stay there and hold on to him. His name's Ringer, by the way.'

Ringer, hearing his name, suddenly decided to leave Addy and she had a real job to hold him, but she clung on somehow, made more determined, she thought afterwards, by the muffled laughter from above her head. Lance might think it awfully funny as she was dragged hither and thither round the yard, but it was not his knuckles which got skinned on the paint-room stairs, nor his arms being pulled out of their sockets.

But help really was at hand. A short, stocky man with grey hair and very light blue eyes came across the courtyard. He was shaking his head and sighing, and as soon as Ringer caught sight of him his thin, whippy little tail began to beat frantically and his barrel-like body with its gleaming brindled coat began to undulate with pleasure.

'Ringer, how did ye get away, old lad?' Ned Armstrong said. 'Thanks very much, love, for catching him. He's on guard duty tonight; I'm opening the kiln after-hours, to take a consignment out, so he'll keep me company.' Addy released the dog's collar and Ringer leapt up at his owner, licking any bit of bare skin he could reach. 'Who's a cunning old bastard, then?'

Ned continued. 'How did ye escape, eh? That's what we're after knowing!'

Addy guessed as soon as she saw which of the cars on the park belonged to Mr Armstrong, since the window was more than half-open, but she said nothing and Ned and the bounding Ringer made off and Addy went up to the paint-room to rescue Bunty.

'She'll be all right here until you go home,' Beryl said comfortably, however, when Addy suggested taking her back right away. 'I've given her some milk and she's settled down, so she'll be fine for a couple of hours.'

When Lance and Addy met at half-past five, she was clutching Bunty and told him that their plans would have to be changed a bit.

'But why don't you come home with me, and have tea at my place and then we can go on to the cinema after I've visited Mum?' she said, both arms round the cat, which was struggling grimly, apparently under the impression that Addy had evil intentions. 'Oh, lor, she's going to get away in a minute.'

Lance silently took the cat, gripping her in a firm but kindly fashion, her front paws trapped in one hand and her rear half tucked beneath his arm. Bunty promptly stopped struggling and began to purr.

'Thanks, that's a good idea,' he said, heading for the car-park. 'Look, I'll have to give Angela a ring though. She wanted me to do some work in the garden this evening and I've not had a chance to tell her I won't be around. Can we put Bunty inside the car and then go back into the museum to ring?'

'You go; I'll wait with Bunty,' Addy said, but Lance was having none of it.

'You don't know Angela; she'll probably ask to speak to you, just to make sure the invitation's genuine or something. Oh, come on, be a sport.'

So Addy went back with him, fishing her purse out of her bag whilst Lance rang, to check that she had enough money for a takeaway. She had, because she had albeit reluctantly, accepted Beryl's offered loan. But just as she heard Lance say, 'She's here, Angela, if you want . . . no, all right. No, I understand . . .' she dropped her bag upside down on the foyer floor and had to scrabble for the contents amongst the display cases and book racks, finding things everywhere and piling them on the counter until she could stuff them back into her bag.

Afterwards, she wondered if she had done it on purpose, so that she would not have to listen to what Lance was saying. But that sounded so fanciful and silly that she dismissed the thought. Still, she certainly had not heard anything after the bag went down and was able to say so when Lance said he hoped she had noticed how firm he had been with his parent.

'She's got to learn that I'm old enough to manage my own affairs,' he said as they went back to the car. 'She says she relies on me, and then cross-questions me about every move I make!'

They reached Addy's house rather later than they had intended, and as soon as the door was opened Bunty simply leapt out, rushed up the path and disappeared. Addy searched half-heartedly, but she wanted to get to the hospital in good time so gave in to Lance's urgings to leave the cat and see to her later, after the hospital visit.

'You're right; she's happier outside than in, unless I'm staying with her,' Addy admitted. 'If we're going to get to the cinema on time though, we'll have to postpone our meal until after the show.'

'Doesn't worry me,' Lance said. 'We'll have hot-dogs in the interval, and lots of icecream and popcorn and crisps and peanuts and . . .'

Addy laughed, the car roared, and they were off, to the hospital.

Sometimes, hospital visiting isn't the easiest thing in the world; you have to make conversation for an hour to someone you may scarcely know at all or, in Addy's case, to someone you know so well that you can think of nothing new to say. But this evening she was bubbling with the story of Bunty and the dog so that she burst into her mother's side ward with words already on her lips.

And found it empty, the bedclothes gone, the mattress bare. For a moment the most ghastly misgiving stopped her dead in her tracks, her heart descending into her sandals. Had something awful happened? Surely Mum could not – could not –

'Hello, love. Come to visit Mrs Bates, have you?'

It was a young nurse, all curls and clean pink dress, smiling at her. 'It's all right, don't look so stunned, she was so much better she's been moved into the main ward – fifth bed on the right.'

The main ward was huge, the beds filled with every age and type of woman, but Addy's eyes homed in on her mother at once and she felt a big smile spread across her face. Mum was looking so much better! Her hair had been washed and her face was made up and, what was more, she was wearing her prettiest nightie – a sure sign of imminent recovery. She beamed at her daughter, her face softening with an affection she rarely showed.

'Hello, Addy, nice to see you. Feeling more like meself I am, full of beans, see? And no drip, either.' She pointed to her bare arm. 'Well, what've you brought me?'

Addy smiled at the cheerful, almost child-like note in her mother's voice and produced her presents.

'Chocolates from Lance. He says get well soon so's he can meet you. A nice fat paperback book in case you feel like a bit of a read – that's from me. Some grapes, they're from Bunty, and a big bottle of scent from the girls in your department. Did Edna come? She said she'd told your feller, Stanley Whatshisname, and he was going to come and visit you.'

At the mere mention of a man, Mum's hands went to her hair, bouncing up the ends. She smiled dotingly past Addy at her own reflection in the windowpane.

'Yes, she's been, and I know she told him because he left a message to say he couldn't come tonight, doing overtime or something, but he'll come tomorrow and bring me something nice. I told him it 'ud better be good, since he's missed seeing me in the side ward, when we could have been a bit more private, but I'm not sorry really. I'd rather he saw me at me best. Now, tell me how you been managing.'

Addy told the tale of desperate Bunty and pursuing Ringer and had the pleasure of seeing her mother show first genuine amusement and then genuine concern. She was really fond of the cat, there was no doubt about that – and of me, too, Addy told herself as her mother hissed in her breath at the moment in the story where Addy had fallen on the bull-terrier.

'You were lucky,' she said impressively when the tale had been told. 'That Ringer, he's trained to kill, I've heard Ned Armstrong say so many a time.'

'He didn't show much sign of it, except with Bunty,' Addy said cheerfully. 'Now shall I tell you about Lance's mother?'

That story also took time, with Mrs Bates exclaiming over the wonderful house and the wonderful meal and looking thoughtful when Addy told her how hard Mrs Peterson worked Lance and how little, when it came down to it, she seemed to appreciate him.

'Takes all sorts,' she said at last, leaning back on her pillows. 'I'm easy-going, you'll give me that, eh, gal?'

'Yes, you're easy-going,' Addy said, smiling at her. 'And you aren't terribly interested in cooking either, are you Mum?'

'Not all that much,' agreed her mother. 'But I don't drive you round the bend do I, gal? That lad of yours could do a lot worse.'

Addy was so surprised she nearly let it show, but instead she just smiled and said she was not too sure that Lance was her lad, exactly.

'He's good fun,' she said. 'So I guess we'll hang out together until the autumn.'

'And work? You've not mentioned work.'

'It's rather boring,' Addy said carefully. 'I'm not sure I can stand it for the rest of my life, Mum. I'll maybe look round for something different in a few months.'

'Oh, well. Maybe you could get a job in a shop? Woolies would be nice, or that *Mates* place you youngsters seem so fond of.'

'We'll see. Mum, I'm going to try to tidy the garden up a bit. And if you like, I'll have a go at decorating, as well.'

Her mother shrugged. She was looking rather tired now, Addy saw with concern.

'Oh, why bother? We only sleep there, when all's said and done.'

'Yes, but I think we ought to try a bit harder, Mum.'

'I don't see it. If it matters to you whether the washing-up gets done once a day or once a week, then that's different, but it doesn't matter to me. I like to eat, I like to sleep, I like the bed made every now and then . . . I mean the house is clean, wouldn't you say?'

'We-ll, if you want the truth . . .'

'Rubbish, course it's clean! Well, fairly clean. I won't pretend it's tidy – it won't be tidy, but it's clean. I hoover sometimes, don't I? And I wash up whenever the crocks run out.'

'So you do. But we ought to keep the garden tidy, and we ought to clean up the outside, shouldn't we? Just the front door, perhaps.'

'It's the council who do things like that, and it's done me for years, so it can do a few more,' her mother said firmly. 'Look, we're working gals now, the pair of us. We need to play as well,

101

and now you've decided to get grown-up it'll be easier, we'll have two lots of money coming in. We could pay someone to do bits and bobs about the place.'

Addy took a deep breath, then exhaled without saying anything. She knew she couldn't stand the paint-room for months and months, she just knew it! And she loved drawing and painting. She wished she had never agreed so meekly to give up all thought of art college and go straight into the pottery. When September came and Lance went back to his college and Betty was permanently in the museum, guiding, she would be bored to tears. But she was supposed to like the idea of working for her living, painting identical poppies on identical mugs. There must be more to life than that, she thought desperately, on the very verge of upsetting her mother by making a wild statement. But then Mum started talking again and Addy put her rebellion out of her mind, for the moment at any rate.

'I may be in another four or five days,' Mrs Bates said. 'So come tomorrow, won't you, and bring that lad of yours, that Lance. Tell you what, come at the usual time and I'll get Stan to come then as well and we can all of us have a good old chat. Oh, you'll like my Stan . . . Jacko, his pals call him. . . he's a real card. Hey, Addy, you all right, chuck?'

Addy stared at her mother; she hoped she had not heard right.

'Did you say Stan was called Jacko, Mum? And he works in Despatch?'

'That's him. Why, do you know him?' Her mother's placid expression suddenly sharpened and a narrow-eyed look took its place. 'He's not been sniffing round you, has he? Just because I'm stuck in here he's not been . . .'

'Mum, honestly, as if anyone would! No, I've never met him but someone mentioned a Jacko, in Despatch. I didn't realize they were talking about your Stan.'

'What did they say?' Her mother was looking bright-eyed and interested again, the jealousy – if that was what it had been – dissipated as soon as she had heard Addy's denial. 'They all know Jacko, at the pot-bank, he's sharp as a needle is my Stan. If you want something just mention it to Jacko, they say, and ten to one he'll fix it for you. Aye, that's my Stan.'

'He sounds great fun,' Addy said hollowly. 'I must fly now, Mum. See you tomorrow, then.'

'That's right, see you tomorrow,' Lila Bates said. She leaned back on her pillows, her eyelids heavy; clearly the hour allowed for visiting was all she could manage as yet. 'See you tomorrow then, chuck.'

All the way back to the car, Addy wondered harder than ever just what Jacko was implicated in. Perhaps it was nothing . . . but her mother had implied in every word she said that Jacko – Stan – was a sharp sort of person, up to anything. Addy was still interested in that overheard conversation, of course, but in her heart she was beginning to think it was nothing much more than the making of a little illicit money on the side, probably from the sale of a bit more china than the pot-bank knew it was producing.

But millions? Why would that fellow have said millions?

She was in the car and fastening the safety-belt when she remembered something else. She put a detaining hand on Lance's arm.

'Hang on a minute, would you? There was something I noticed today, something odd, only the dog and Bunty and everything put it out of my head. Lance, you know the disused kiln?'

'Yup,' Lance said. 'Well, I don't know any more about it than that it is disused. It's empty, so I don't have to clean in there or anything.'

'It isn't. Well, there was a man in it this dinner-time because . . .'

Addy told the story of her near-miss with the man, the dim glimpse she had caught of the interior of the kiln, and the man's prompt and total disappearance. Lance heard her out and then he said bluntly, 'He can't have come out of that kiln. They've lost the key to it, I heard someone saying the other day. I expect you were in such a hurry that you just *thought* he came out of there . . . got the impression he did. You know how it can happen.'

'No I don't. I'm observant – you've got to be if you're going to draw – and I know what I saw and where I saw it,' Addy assured him. 'That guy was in the kiln and he dodged back in as soon as he saw me.'

'Well, if he was in there, then something really is going on,' Lance said. 'Tomorrow I'll snoop round there, see whether I can see anything.'

'Yes . . . but Lance, there's one more thing.'

'What? Don't say Ringer is a spy!'

His tone annoyed Addy; he still only half believed in the man in the kiln, she could tell. He was almost humouring her. She debated for a

104

second whether to tell him about Jacko, and then he laughed, leaned over and kissed the side of her face, and she laughed too.

'Sorry if I'm being touchy . . . but listen to this!'

Lance, to do him credit, looked far more serious over the revelation that Jacko was, in fact, Stanley Jackson, Lila Bates's latest boyfriend.

'Hell! And I suppose even if we do discover what they're up to, you won't want to do anything about it!'

'Yes, I shall. I don't know this man at all myself, and Mum won't shed many tears if he's a real wrong 'un,' Addy said stoutly, but with secret doubts. 'You go ahead, Lance, and have a good pry tomorrow; I'm sure you'll find out I'm right!'

But at this point Lance glanced at his watch and started the car with a jerk.

'We'll miss the beginning,' he groaned, putting his foot down hard to the floor. 'Hang on, Addy, we're going to shift ourselves.'

'It was a good film,' Addy said later that evening, as they emerged from the cinema into the deep summer dusk. 'What'll it be? Chinese, Indian or fish and chips?'

They settled for a chinese curry each, then Lance drove her home and they both got out. Bunty was waiting for them, a patient figure fatly squatting beside the front door. Addy fumbled for her key, then, failing to find it, crouched on the front path and emptied the bag out on to the cracked and weedy concrete.

'It's got to be here somewhere,' she muttered. 'It's odd, I always keep it with my purse so that . . .'

Her voice faded away. She stared up at Lance, feeling the colour drain from her face.

'Oh, damn!'

'What have you done with it?' Lance asked. 'Is it at the hospital? Didn't you get it out when you brought Bunty home?'

'No . . . oh, Lance, you'll never guess! It's in the museum foyer, on the long counter. When you were telephoning home I dropped my bag, do you remember, and all the things rolled everywhere. I picked up the keys and everything else and piled it all on the counter, but I left the keys until last so they'd be near the top . . . and I don't remember picking them up! They're still there, and I'm locked out!'

They ate the chinese curries whilst they discussed what they should do. Lance wanted Addy to return to his house for the night but Addy felt she could not just land herself on Mrs Peterson, and Lance, though perfectly willing, indeed rather eager, to ring her, did not bother to hide the fact that Mrs Peterson hated to be woken up.

'Besides, I want to go home in case the hospital ring or something,' Addy said, suddenly desperate for her own small bed and Bunty's comfortable weight on her toes. 'And then all my clean clothes for tomorrow are in there . . . let's see if I left a window open.'

She knew she hadn't. She was too aware of the responsibility of being in charge to have done such a thing. And she also disliked Bunty's dirty habits, so had even closed the window-light in the kitchen.

'I'll break in, if you like,' Lance whispered, but Addy told him quite sharply not to be so silly

– the neighbours might all be in bed but they would soon wake at the sound of breaking glass, and then she and he might well find themselves spending the night in a police cell.

'You can just drive me back to the museum,' she said at last. 'And lend me your keys. It won't take a second, I'll just unlock, grab my things, and lock up again. I won't ask you to come as well, in case you think it's illegal or something.'

'Fool! We'll both go,' Lance said. In the greeny light from the streetlamp his face looked wickedly delighted. 'What a chance, eh? We'll walk slap into the ghost, see if we don't. Wheee-eeee!'

'I don't believe that ghosts have to appear after dark,' Addy said. She folded her foil container and took Lance's as well, then dropped them into the pocket in the car door. 'Will you really use your keys to get us in? Oh, thanks, Lance, you've saved my life.'

'Not yet, I haven't,' Lance said, starting the car. 'You may die of terror as ghostly fingers clutch your throat.'

'And you may die of my unghostly fingers clutching at your throat,' Addy said crossly. 'Just shut up about ghosts – I say, what about taking a look round the kiln whilst we're there?'

'I don't know about that,' Lance said. 'I wouldn't hesitate for a moment to use my keys to get your property back, and if you do feel you'd like to peep into the delft-room whilst you're in there, why not? I mean, I could say you thought you'd left your keys in there. But snooping about in the courtyard could be a bit chancy.'

'Well, wait and see,' Addy said. 'I just hope the bobby on the beat doesn't turn up at an unfortunate moment.'

Lance laughed and drew into a parking space, for they had already reached the street which housed the museum.

'It's pretty quiet,' he murmured, as they got out of the car. 'Sure you want to go ahead with it?'

'Certain sure.'

'Right on, ma'am. Here we go, then.'

They crossed the road. It was very dark and still, the streetlamps casting pools of orange light here in the town centre. Nothing moved, not even a cat, and the museum itself was in deep shadow, not a light illuminating the imposing frontage.

'Gates first,' Lance said briskly. He unlocked them, swung one inwards, then closed and locked it behind him. 'Not fair to the authorities to leave it unlocked,' he murmured in her ear. 'If someone was to break in . . .' he chuckled, leaving the sentence open.

They had only twenty or so metres to cross to reach the shelter of the big open-fronted porch but here, for some reason, it was Addy who hung back. All of a sudden the building looked very big and strange and even a bit frightening. She felt unwanted there, an intruder on the secret life of the place. She clutched Lance's arm.

'Should we?' Addy murmured. 'Oh, Lance, perhaps you were right and we ought not.'

'Gone too far now to turn back,' Lance said. He pushed his key into the lock, undid the door, leaned through the doorway and pushed a switch up, then pulled her inside and locked the door again, behind them.

'Wh-what was that switch?' Addy quavered. Her heart was working overtime. 'Wh-why did you touch it?'

'Burglar alarm. I do it each morning; cancel it, so it doesn't go off and scare the pants off anyone passing. Here, shall I put the lights on? Might as well search in comfort.'

'No!' Addy hissed. 'Not the lights . . . honestly, we don't need them, I know more or less exactly where I put those keys.'

Lance laughed beneath his breath. Mockingly, but with a tiny catch in the laugh which told Addy that he was as tense as she was.

'More or less exactly! Just like a woman! Come on, then – to the foyer.'

They reached the foyer without a fumble or misstep because of the moonlight flooding in through the side window, and in the foyer itself Addy pounced at once on her keys, shining silvery and reliable just where she had put them down on the long counter.

'Got them! Can we go now?'

'Go? We've only just arrived.' Lance took her hand, his fingers warm, confident. Addy felt a lot better like that. If a ghost does suddenly appear, she told herself, at least we can both run at it, waving our arms and shrieking. Probably it would turn and run faster than us if that happened.

'To the delft-room,' Lance said. He sounded happy, self-confident. Clearly, though he had been against the idea at the start, having taken the first step he was now eager to continue with what he obviously regarded as a challenge. 'Come on, Addy, or the witching hour of midnight will find us still dithering here.'

'Midnight!' Addy glanced at her watch and saw that it was indeed five to twelve, and suddenly she found herself as keen as Lance to go through with it. Not many people had the chance to be in a haunted room at exactly midnight, in a building a couple of hundred years old, with someone who claimed to have seen the ghost once already!

Nevertheless, as they entered the delft-room, she did find herself clinging rather closely to Lance, and did not object at all when he put his arm round her.

'In we go,' he murmured against her ear. 'Listen hard, and keep your eyes peeled!'

He opened the door slowly, pushing it gently so that it scarcely made a sound. Indeed, far louder than the noise of the door's movement, louder than their combined breathing, even louder than the thump of Addy's heart, was the sound of the distant town hall clock, striking midnight.

6

With the door open, Addy and Lance could see the length of the room even in the dark, with the moonlight making things more difficult by casting brilliant white light in one place and black shadow in another.

The mirror-backed cases showed their white faces – white from moonlight, not from fear, Addy reminded herself – and the reflection of the china, other cases, the windows . . .

Movement! Addy knew Lance had seen it too, because his arm tightened around her, then relaxed, but only a little.

'Someone's in the courtyard,' he murmured. 'A man . . . can you see him?'

'Yes,' Addy whispered after a moment. 'Not one man, though; two. They're moving, they'll be out of sight in a tick.'

She was right, but Lance was moving almost as quickly, pulling the door of the delft-room nearly shut and taking her at a jog-trot back down the corridor to the main foyer, with its glazed doors leading out into the courtyard on one side, and the corridor which led to the main entrance on the other.

'Did we see a ghost?' Addy hissed doubtfully, as they reached the large foyer and stopped for a moment. 'It looked like a chap in a boiler suit to me. I reckon someone's working late.'

Lance raised his brows and grinned down at her.

'That was no ghost – I can't be sure until I've taken a peep through this half-door, but it looked like . . .' He peered through the glass in the top half of the door, then turned triumphantly back to Addy. 'It's that fellow your mum knows – Jacko, from Despatch!'

'Mum said he was working late,' Addy said. 'Can it be legitimate work after all, Lance?'

'Late? Addy, use your loaf. It's well after midnight, you heard the clock striking, and they aren't anywhere near the renovated kiln, they're after the old one – you can see the way they're walking.'

'Ye-es,' Addy agreed after a pause during which she also stared through the glass. 'Ooh, look!'

The door of the old kiln must have opened for it spilled warm, honey-coloured light across the grass for an instant, then the flood of light changed to a trickle as the door half closed.

'I reckon they're all inside,' Lance said, his hand on the doorknob. 'I'm going to take a look – coming?'

If there was one thing Addy did not fancy, it was being left there, in that old building which might or might not contain a ghost but which was certainly spooky enough at midnight to make you wonder.

'I'm right behind you,' she said fervently. 'What'll we do?'

'Get as near the old kiln as we can,' Lance said. 'Keep under cover – there are masses of bushes and tall grass. If I want you to stop I'll squeeze your hand.'

They were still holding hands but this, unfortunately, proved to be impossible once they began wending their way through the bushes. Addy kept close at Lance's heels, though, ready to grab him if she saw something which he did not, and when he stopped she was able to stop immediately, as well, before there was a collision.

'Stay here,' Lance said at one point. 'I'm just going to nip across to the door . . .'

They came round the corner of a tangled mass of gorse and broom and saw the doorway, faintly outlined with light. And the covered lorry, standing there. Lance drew back, which was as well since even as they watched two men emerged from the kiln carrying what looked like quite a small box between them.

It looked too small to need two, but a snatch of conversation rang in Addy's head, making sense of it.

'It weighs heavy, of course.'

One of the voices over the intercom had said that, and this, whatever it was, certainly seemed to confirm what the man had said. The small box was clearly very heavy indeed, and the men grunted and muttered to each other and then dumped the box in the back of the lorry with a muffled thud.

Lance waited until the men had disappeared once more into the kiln and then nudged Addy.

'Stay here. I'm going to take a look.'

113

'They'll be back in a moment . . . oh, Lance, be careful,' Addy hissed in agonized apprehension. But Lance only squeezed her fingers and then shot off, heading straight for the back of the lorry. Addy stayed where she was, her heart hammering, but before the kiln door had opened again Lance was back, his eyes very bright in the moonlight, his mouth curved in a happy grin.

'You'll never guess, Addy! It's little bars of metal! Each bar's about the size of two squares of chocolate . . . but I think it's gold!'

'Gold?' But even as she tried to whip up some disbelief, Addy found herself believing it. It made sense of the weight, the relatively small quantity the man had mentioned . . . and especially the bit about being millionaires. But . . . legal? Surely enough gold to make anyone a million quid must be stolen?

'Well, I can't be sure, but it really looks like gold ingots. Look, Addy, I dared not take one out of the box in case they check, but I think we ought to get out of here and go to the police. Are you game to slither back?'

Addy was about to agree when the door opened again and two men emerged. This time Addy recognized Mr Braithwaite from Personnel, though the man with him was a stranger to her. And then she recognized someone else. A someone with a wide grin, excellent teeth and slit eyes.

Ringer!

The men were talking amongst themselves, calling back to someone still inside the kiln, and Ringer was sniffing unconcernedly around the base of it, cocking his leg against the brickwork, sniffing a bit further, then angling away from the

114

kiln towards the very clump of bushes which hid Addy and Lance.

He came nearer, nearer . . .

You could see that he was following a scent, and Addy realized that it was very probably Lance's trail, where her companion had run forward to see what was in the lorry and then retraced his steps. Ringer wasn't looking particularly fierce, or no fiercer than usual, anyway, but he looked both interested and determined.

He was within two metres of them when Lance bent, fumbled, and then brought his arm back and up. Addy could not imagine what he was doing until she saw the stone arc up into the sky and come down, none too quietly, on the opposite side of the yard.

The dog spun round, stared, and then set off at the only sort of gallop such short legs could manage, but it was fast enough for Addy to know without a shadow of doubt that if she and Lance ran for the museum, Ringer would get there first. Or rather, he would get them first.

'When he's not looking I'm going to make for the courtyard, try to reach the museum doors,' Lance whispered, his mouth close to Addy's ear. 'Want to have a go as well?'

'No point,' Addy hissed back. 'If you're caught then there's still me, hidden here, to have my try. You go, but wait until the dog's called back into the kiln. Or at least until he's forgotten what he was doing before you threw the stone.'

They might have had a long wait, but for Ringer himself. He had fetched the stone, but since he had no idea who had thrown it he naturally trotted up to the first person he could see, which was his master, emerging from the kiln on one end of another small but heavy box. Ringer bounced up to him, dropped the stone, lowered his front half to the ground, cocked up his ample bottom, and whimpered expectantly. Even across the intervening space, Addy could hear the desperation in Ned Armstrong's forceful but lowered tones.

'Shut it, Ringer, you stupid beggar! Get back in . . . d'you hear me? *Get in!*'

And to the relief of far more people than he supposed, Ringer sighed but picked up his stone and obeyed, trotting docilely into the kiln and round the corner, out of sight. The two men dumped the latest box into the back of the lorry and followed the dog back into the kiln. The door closed behind them.

'Now,' Lance said. 'If you're staying, get well into the bushes; if you're coming, come now.'

Addy hesitated; she was very tempted, but she felt strongly that she ought to stay. Suppose it took Lance longer to bring the police than it took the men to load the rest of the gold? Then no one would know where they had gone, unless someone was there to see at least what direction they left in, perhaps even follow them.

'You go,' she said finally. 'I'll keep watch.'

Lance squeezed her hand and set off, without more ado, across the courtyard.

He moved quickly and quietly, a shadow amongst shadows. Addy saw him reach the museum, slip through the glazed doors, half raise a hand in her direction and then close the door softly behind him. For her part, she just pressed more deeply into her bushes. Never had she felt so alone and exposed. But she was there for a purpose – she must watch!

Presently, she was rewarded. The men opened the door wide so that they could begin bringing the boxes out a couple at a time, and they also brought out two cylinders on a trolley. Without quite knowing what made her think of it, Addy found that she was remembering heat was important, and she knew, then, what she was looking at. It was oxy-acetylene equipment and it could be used to melt metal, so hotly could the jets burn.

What was more, she remembered where she had last seen it, before it had turned up here, in the old kiln.

It had been in the miner's hut, out on the moors!

Pressed in her prickly nest, Addy spent a while just thinking things out, clarifying them in her own mind. The men had begged, borrowed or stolen the oxy-acetylene equipment to erase something from the gold bars, she presumed identification marks of some sort, and they had hidden the equipment in the miner's hut until the time was ripe to use it.

Now the bars were clear of the marks though, they would move them away from the pottery, because it couldn't be too safe. Sooner or later someone in authority would want to get into the old kiln, would demand that the key be found. Already it was being remarked upon, so Lance had said, that the key had disappeared.

And where would they take the bars? Where else but to the miner's hut? She wondered why they had not taken the bars there first and done the work on them there too, then remembered that anyone passing by on the road above and looking down would get a clear view, through the gaps in the slates, of lights, or the glow from the equipment. What was more, she had no idea how the hut would stand up to fierce heat, whereas the kiln had been built to withstand very high temperatures. So that would be why the gold had been fired here, rather than in the miner's hut.

But this is all guesswork, Addy reminded herself, as the men came out with the boxes and went back in for more. I'm trying to interpret facts without enough knowledge, really. But if I had to make a guess, that's what it would be.

Time passed and the little boxes of gold piled higher and higher in the lorry. There was no sign of Lance. He won't have locked up in case I decided to follow him, Addy told herself. Now that I'm nearly sure I know where the gold will end up, shouldn't I make a break for it? Shouldn't I try to get out, too? The run across the courtyard was some distance, but perfectly possible provided she waited until the men had just delivered a box.

She began to wriggle forward until she was almost clear of the bushes, then hesitated because all four of the men had emerged. They were talking quietly, pushing the tailboard of the lorry up, adjusting the canvas doors at the back. She could see someone, she thought it was Jacko, with a broom, clearing the floor. Doubtless they were erasing the slightest trace of their presence before leaving the old kiln.

Addy stuck her hands in her pockets, and her fingers encountered a crumpled piece of paper, a roll of mints, a stub of pencil. For something to do she pulled out the piece of paper and found it was her sketch of Lance, falling into the stream the other Sunday outside the miner's hut.

If the worst happens and they catch me, I can leave this as a clue for Lance, Addy told herself. But they would not catch her, because she had no intention of doing anything brave, like moving out of cover. Still, she dropped the sketch behind the bushes, then moved forward so that she might hear what the men were talking about, just in case it proved useful.

'We're off now, then,' Mr Braithwaite remarked, locking the door of the kiln and heading for the lorry. 'Unlock the gate and we'll be away. It's late, but it's work as usual tomorrow, chaps.'

Everyone laughed, but Ned said: 'I'll just let Ringer out for a run; he's been in a while, better let him raise his leg.'

'Aye, better here than in the lorry,' Jacko said, grinning. Addy, eyeing him curiously, could see why her mother was attracted to the man. He was tall and flashy-looking, with dark, rather long hair which waved around his ears and a cocky grin, but he also had a jaunty air, as if he relished the darkness, the adventure of it all. The other men plainly wanted to get out and get away, but Jacko, Addy thought, would be sorry when it was all over and life went back to normal, even if he was a great deal richer.

'Come on, old boy,' Ned said. He opened the kiln door and the dog trotted out. 'Seek 'em out, then . . . get your legs moving, old son.'

Ringer looked around him, and seemed to see Addy without a shadow of a doubt. He stiffened, growled beneath his breath . . . and

119

then came towards her like a bullet from a gun.

Afterwards, Addy was inclined to believe that if she had held her ground and stayed very still she might have fooled him into believing her to be just another shadow. He had not given her the impression, in their earlier encounters, of being a dog overburdened with brains. But, in fact, with what looked like half a ton of teeth bearing down upon her she broke cover and ran for the museum. If she could just get inside . . .

The men were surprised, she could hear it in their voices as they shouted to each other and to Ringer.

'Keep still, lad, or he'll have you,' Ned bawled, but the moonlight made it difficult for them to see her clearly and she was halfway to the door, in full, terrified flight with Ringer's hot breath on the backs of her legs, when the dog, for some reason best known to himself, suddenly abandoned the chase. He gave a series of little yelps, each one higher than the last, and then ran like the wind away from her, back towards the old kiln, howling as he went.

Addy, still running, thought that someone was coming out from the museum towards her, someone smallish, with long brown hair and a draggly sort of skirt, but she barely caught a glimpse before the other girl was dodging past and round her, apparently heading straight for the pursuing men.

'There's two of 'em, a lad and a lass. Get that bloody dog going!' shouted Mr Braithwaite. Addy recognized the plummy voice even when it was sharpened by fear and malice. But as she dodged into another patch of shadow she could see Ringer in full flight, heading for the lorry, his tail tucked so far between his legs that he looked like a Manx cat. And in the patches of white light and black shadow, Addy and the girl she never quite saw dodged and ran and dodged again, getting even nearer the museum doors.

Addy reached it, actually had her fingers on the handle, when she was seized from behind and lifted off her feet.

'Gotcher!' said a breathless voice with a local accent. 'Caught, young feller . . . now we'll get the little lass!'

It was Jacko.

'There were two of 'em, this one's a lass in jeans, the other was a lass in a skirt,' Jacko kept insisting, long after they had surrounded Addy, with Jacko still holding her wrist in an iron grip. 'Didn't you see the little lass? Come on, you must have seen her.'

But no one had, or at least, no one admitted to it.

'It's the moonlight, and this lassie moved so fast she looked like two,' Ned Armstrong said. 'Och, Jacko, it was just the one; or are you trying to say the other got away?'

'I'd like to know how you got in,' Mr Braithwaite said, sounding peevish. 'How did you get in? We locked up after us, I'd swear.'

'I left my front-door key in work, so I climbed over the back wall,' Addy said sullenly. 'My mum's in hospital and I'd been to the cinema only when I got home I couldn't get in, so I came over the wall.'

'You did?' Jacko was staring at her with a mixture of admiration and disbelief. 'That wall's four metres high and topped with broken glass!'

'I bashed the glass flat with a brick and put my coat on it,' Addy said, keeping her voice cross rather than frightened. 'Why shouldn't I? I work here too, you know.'

'How did you climb four metres?' Jacko countered. 'Any road, we're here official-like, on business.'

'There's a tree near the wall, the other side,' Addy said, hoping they wouldn't find it necessary to check. 'What does it matter, anyway? If you'll just let me go you can watch me disappear in a puff of smoke, if that's how you think I got in!'

Jacko grinned but Mr Braithwaite did not think it amusing.

'You've no right here,' he said pompously. 'We should hand you over to the authorities for trespassing.'

Addy held her breath; that would suit her just fine! But then another voice spoke, the voice of the man she had not recognized, had in fact not yet seen properly. He called out from the kiln.

'I think she'd better come with us. I dare say she's already taken a look at our lorry load.'

Considering she was pressed up against the tailboard, this was a fair guess, but Addy shook her head.

'No, I haven't,' she insisted stoutly. 'I'm not interested. Anyway, why shouldn't I see what you've got in the lorry, if you're here officially?'

As soon as the words were out, she regretted them. What a stupid thing to say – it was as though she was daring them to lie again, or to tell her the truth and involve her so deeply that they would not dare to let her go.

The voice from the unseen man in the kiln came again.

'If she was just picking up her key then what was she doing hiding in those bushes? Because she *was* hiding. And when the dog rushed at her she didn't stand still, or make for the wall, she ran for the museum. We'll have to take her with us.'

Jacko had been grinning, pleased with himself for having caught her, hyped up, she thought, by the excitement of the whole thing. Now, as she watched, the grin faded. He looked suddenly wretched, almost frightened.

'Take her with us? But we aren't going nowhere!'

The man in the kiln sighed exaggeratedly, then said briefly, 'Put her in the lorry. Tie her ankles and wrists, we don't want her running off.'

Addy would have run then, but Ned Armstrong was already kneeling, tying her ankles, whilst Mr Braithwaite, muttering under his breath, rather inexpertly did the same with her wrists.

'Now . . . up with you,' Ned said, and Addy found herself hoisted over the tailboard of the lorry and dumped unceremoniously down to one side of the pile of boxes. Ned grabbed a pile of sacks and covered her up with them. 'No point in shouting: if you do, we'll have to gag you,' he said briefly. You won't be here long, it's not far to . . . to where we're going.'

He jumped down off the lorry and closed the back so that Addy was lying in darkness. Presently, the lorry started up. It bumped and bounced, slowed, speeded up, and through the numerous cracks in the bodywork Addy could see street lighting, then the occasional house, then the soft dark of open country.

The lorry travelled on. And presently, after what seemed an awfully long time to Addy, it stopped, then started again. Then it stopped and the engine was switched off. Voices were heard . . . and the night noises of small birds, disturbed. And the chuckling of a stream.

We're there, Addy told herself, but although the men let the tailboard of the lorry down nothing seemed to be happening and presently, astonishingly, Addy fell asleep.

Addy woke because someone was shaking her. It was broad daylight; clearly she had slept the night away. She opened her eyes and rolled over, looking straight up into a man's face. It was a bit of a shock to find that he was wearing a stocking-mask which turned him into an anonymous horror, but she knew it was the man she had not seen. At least, since it was neither Ned, Jacko or Mr Braithwaite, she assumed that the mask must hide the identity of the man who had lurked in the kiln and given orders when she had been captured.

'All right, are you? Recognize me? Of course you don't, not through this, so you might as well come along out of it.'

It was the same cultured, accentless voice which she had heard the previous night, and now he picked her up as though she weighed nothing and carried her out of the lorry, setting her down on the ground as they reached it.

'Come on,' Ned growled at her. Ringer pranced up and down beside his master, nuzzling Addy. She was not sure that she liked this apparently affectionate greeting – who knew whether he was inspecting her for later dinners? What was more, her progress could be nothing short of laughable with her ankles tied. Her shuffle merely clouded dust up round her feet and made Ringer back away and yap, blinking his slitty eyes.

'Untie her ankles, you fool,' the man in the stocking-mask said tersely. 'There's nowhere here for her to run.'

Once her ankles were free, Addy realized she could walk all right though her legs were black and blue, and she tottered rather unsteadily beside Ned round the corner of the lorry. There was the miner's hut, just as she had thought it would be.

'In there,' Ned said, though not unkindly. 'Stay there quiet, there's a good lass, until we've worked things out. Don't go shouting, not that it'll do ye much good away down here. We'll be back later.'

Addy, pushed into the small, square room, said nothing. She leaned against the wall and watched the door close, heard the padlock snap into place and then, quite soon, heard the lorry drive away.

Should I have told them that Lance knew, she wondered, so that they wouldn't think that silencing me would put them in the clear? Or was it sufficient to trust Lance to bring the police? But he had not got back to her last night, and he might never find the crumpled sketch or, even if he found it, might not realize its significance. Piled up against the back of the small room were the boxes of gold and behind them, though covered in canvas, the oxy-acetylene equipment. Surely the men would not have locked her in with the gold had they intended to allow her to go free to say what she had seen?

Presently, she took a good look at the boxes, for although the hut was windowless, plenty of light was beginning to come in through the cracks around the door and the gaps in the slates overhead. It was reassuring to discover that they were nailed down far too firmly for someone without tools or indeed free hands to prise the lids up, and they were marked in big black letters – HANDLE WITH CARE: PORCELAIN.

So was it possible that they would simply keep her shut away until they were well clear? It was a nice thought, but how could she be fool enough to believe it? They were ordinary men in ordinary jobs, not super-crooks. They wouldn't have planned to take their share of the money and fly off to Argentina or somewhere; they would have planned to buy bigger houses and nicer cars and to have holidays on the Continent and to spend without having to think all the time. Look at that Jacko of Mum's. Judging from what Mum had said he was a bit of a twister but popular with other people, good fun to be with. He wouldn't be planning on escaping to foreign parts with his share of the loot, whatever that might be. He'd be planning to buy Mum a huge box of chocolates or a frilly nightie. Small-time, that described Jacko to a T.

But the big men, Braithwaite and the man in the stocking-mask, they wouldn't risk her telling on them, putting them inside perhaps for years.

126

They wouldn't dare. Whatever they might tell the others she would have to be disposed of, or they'd never sleep soundly in their beds again.

Addy had been leaning against the wall as the sound of the lorry's engine faded and faded, from a deep growl to the faint, high hum of a mosquito. Now she collapsed on to the ground, her knees shaking so much that they could hardly bear her weight.

Would they *kill* her? But that didn't happen to people in real life. In real life . . . even in fiction . . . the cavalry always arrived before the Indians could strike!

It was very quiet in the hut once the lorry's sound had died away. Listening, Addy could hear the stream chattering over its stony bed and a lark bubbling away high in the sky. She knew it must be very early in the morning, so Lance had had hours to find her picture and put two and two together. He would put two and two together, wouldn't he? He would make four, and not five, or half a dozen? Any minute now he would come galloping over the crest of the hill, with his posse behind him, to rescue the Girl Who Knew Too Much.

Just wait quietly and he'll come, Addy said to herself, above the thundering of her heart. There's nothing you can do, anyway, you're locked in, your wrists are tied, and you don't want to antagonize anyone.

Time ticked slowly by. Through the crack in the door post which she had once used to peer in, Addy could see out. The sun was climbing the sky now. It was getting-up time, breakfast-time, time to set out for work.

No one came. Nothing happened. Addy's heart continued to beat so hard that it made her breathless. She was afraid, and scornful of her own fear, but that did not make it less real. She sat on the floor with her arms locked round her knees, trying to become so tiny that she could slide out under the great old door, trying to shrink to nothing.

The sound of an engine on the far-off main road brought her, abruptly, to her senses. She stood up, shook herself, and addressed herself crossly.

'You think they'll kill you, eh? Only Lance will get here in time and save you. Is that it, then? Is that all you're worth? Just a silly little damsel tied up waiting for the dragon . . . with not enough courage to raise a finger to help yourself? Addy Bates, I'm downright ashamed of you!'

Even the sound of her own voice was heartening, she discovered, and courage began to flow through her again. She would *not* sit there and wait for anyone, not Lance or the police or anyone. She would get herself out and go get them!

Easier said than done, Addy.

No. Not easier said than done. Tied wrists were awkward but not impossible. Addy and Diane had once spent an instructive summer holiday binding each other's wrists and then escaping. It had led to some ruined summer-dress belts, and some pretty blunt knives, but they had always got out in the end. Now, Addy looked around her properly, searchingly. There was nothing here but the boxes full of gold and a few broken slates from the roof. The slates wouldn't help much, but if she just leaned against the topmost boxes and rubbed and rubbed . . .

The boxes were rough wood, the rope which bound her old and frayed. Her wrists were free in minutes and Addy looked round for a means of escape. Nothing immediately presented itself until she heard the lark again, its song ascending with trills and runs, and actually saw it, through the holes in the slates.

The roof! But how to reach it? If she could shift the boxes of gold . . . they could then be piled up and she could climb on to them and grab for the roof . . .

The boxes were heavier than Addy had dreamed. She could drag them along the floor, but pile them up she could not. She abandoned that particular escape route, therefore, and looked hopefully at the great door, then at the floor, remembering.

There was a tunnel. It ended, of course . . . but suppose there was some way out? Lance probably hadn't been looking with that in mind, but if she could just get the old lino up . . .

She got it up easily, though she had to tear it right across because of the boxes holding it down one end. And there was the trapdoor, plain as plain. Old, of course, the hinges rusty, but when she heaved it up it came sweetly enough and revealed the dark hole beneath with some steps leading down.

Addy, with trembling haste, descended into darkness. It was horrid. It smelt old and musty and she found she was extremely reluctant to travel the tunnel's length . . . it was bound to be a dead-end, why should she have expected anything else?

But she made herself do it, and it was one of the bravest things she had ever done, going into that pitch-darkness with the smell of decay all around her, one hand held before her to see if she could get out that way.

She went right to the end until her hand met solid rock and her feet, unfortunately, met a scatter of rubble, which meant that her hand met the rock only seconds before her nose met it, too. Warm blood ran, salt-tasting, down her face and Addy felt, all of a sudden, so furiously angry that had the men appeared in the tunnel before her, she would probably have smashed their faces in with whatever lay to hand.

How dared they scare her like that! Who did they think they were, to lock Addy Bates up in a dark place and threaten her? She would show them!

It was in this frame of mind that Addy, bouncing back up the tunnel with her bloody nose aching, saw the steps she had just climbed down without a second thought. They were wooden steps, and they were not attached to the side of the tunnel. They were free-standing, so that when the miner had wanted to take a look at his roof he could get the steps out, lean them against the wall, and climb up them.

Addy, with a grin stretching from ear to ear, climbed up the steps with the speed and agility of a monkey and then turned round and heaved. The steps came up without anything more than a slight clatter as they left the earth into which they had become lightly embedded with the years. Addy leaned them against the nearest wall and shot up them. She reached up to the broken roof and took considerable pleasure in breaking it even further, throwing slates down with gay abandon until the hole was big enough for her to climb right out and sit on the roof ridge, preparing herself to slide down.

It was quite a long way up though, and Addy took advantage of the view to take a good look around. There was a farmhouse above her, but it was still a good way off and in the wrong direction – away from town rather than nearer to it. She could slide down the roof without any real danger if she took care to make a controlled landing, but then she would be in country where she could be seen for about a mile in all directions, until she was up by the main road where there were things like ditches and trees.

She could, of course, stay where she was. She was in a commanding position and could defend herself pretty briskly with the broken slates should anyone attempt to scale the roof to fetch her down. Unless they shot at her . . . Her skin crept at the thought. If they had a gun, she was the sitting target, not them.

But men who worked in pot-banks were unlikely to carry guns. Oh, really? said Addy's cynical side; I dare say they wouldn't wear nylon stocking-masks, or rob gold trains, either? It was no use presuming; she could easily be wrong.

So down it would have to be. She would have to take a chance on rescue being near at hand.

Addy took one last look round and on the main road, far above her, she saw a car, or a lorry, or a truck – she couldn't, from this distance, tell which.

She sat staring, still astride her ridge, in an agony of uncertainty. If it was them then they would recapture her or kill her right here and now. If it wasn't, whoever it was might give her a lift back into town to a police station. If it was Lance . . . but that was too much to hope. She remembered that she had given up on Lance. After all, he'd had all night to do something and just exactly what had he done so far? The guy was useless. In Addy's position he'd never have thought of the roof or the slates!

The vehicle, whatever it was, was turning off from the main road, bouncing and leaping from stone to stone, coming very fast, ignoring the state of its springs or the pressure in its tyres or whatever it was that drivers tend to worry about.

Addy's heart, which had slowed almost to normal, began to speed up again, but her smile stayed firmly in place.

Lance! It was Lance, coming down the old track at a highly dangerous speed to rescue her!

This – Addy thought blissfully, lobbing a slate at random on to the track just for the pleasure of seeing it burst into a dozen pieces – this is the happiest moment of my life!

7

'Jump! I'll catch you! Quick, because I think . . .'
Lance staggered as Addy's weight caught him full
in the chest, but recovered gallantly and stood
her down. 'You must weigh a lot more than you
look . . . Come on, let's get out of here.'

Addy snorted but there was no time for argu-
ing. Lance grabbed her hand and ran her round
to the car. He almost threw her into the passenger seat and then snapped, 'Get down and stay
down!', shot the car into gear and went up the
stony track like a racing-driver.

Curled up in the well at the bottom of the car,
Addy shouted above the wind, 'Why? What's
happening?'

'They're coming down the track,' Lance said,
between gritted teeth. 'It must be them, I recognized the lorry. Just keep your head down and
shut up for once.'

This was not the moment to quibble about
his choice of words, so Addy kept low and said
nothing, but she heard the other vehicle even
above the roar of Lance's overstrained engine as
they tackled the steep slope, bouncing, skidding,
but keeping going even after a really horrible

moment when Lance shouted, 'Hold tight!' and the car seemed to squirm sideways, slithering on loose gravel, and then to right itself and go into orbit. Addy, from her lowly position, could almost imagine the stars streaming past.

The gang, fortunately, were not fussy about shutting gates. The car bucketed through the gateway and then, to Addy's astonishment, Lance stopped, leapt out, tore back, shut and latched the gate and then returned breathlessly to the driver's seat.

If they follow us the gate will hold them up for a few moments, and if they don't it'll be because they think a guy helping someone to escape wouldn't bother to close the gate,' Lance shouted above the whine of the engine as he accelerated on to the main road. 'Phew . . . you can sit up now . . . I say, your face!'

'I bumped my nose on the end of the under-ground passage and made it bleed,' Addy said, sitting up gingerly and rubbing her cramped and aching legs. 'I went down there to see if I could get out that way, and then found the little ladder wasn't attached, so I used it to climb out through the slates and on to the roof. They tied me up, but I got out of the rope . . . I think they meant to bump me off, Lance. I knew too much, what with seeing them bringing the gold out from the kiln and all.'

'Better tell me what happened to you after I left,' Lance said, so Addy filled him in on what had gone on as the car hurtled along the road. Of the chase in the courtyard, however, she gave only the vaguest outline. The second figure she thought she had seen in the patchy moonlight must have been imagination, or wishful thinking, or a combination of both. Yet something had stopped the dog from attacking her. She knew enough about dogs to realize that he would have grabbed her, not being particular over whether it was a mouthful of jeans or a mouthful of leg, in the excitement of the chase, had he not also believed he had seen something strange.

But she said nothing of this to Lance, who listened and nodded.

'So then I got out on to the roof, and I heard an engine, and it was you!' Addy finished, turning her head to smile at him. 'I've never been more pleased to see anyone in my whole life. Now: where were you?'

Lance sighed.

'They say there's never a cop around when you need one, and it's usually true. Did you notice that as we came in I locked the doors behind us, in case of . . . ' he laughed bitterly, ' . . . in case of burglars?'

'I noticed.'

'Well, when I put the keys away I thought I must have done it carelessly, because once I was back inside the museum foyer I put my hand in my pocket and the wretched things weren't there.'

'Cripes!'

'Yeah. So I turned out my pockets and went back to the delft-room for a look around and then remembered that naturally I'd had to unlock the door into the courtyard, and of course the damned things were still in the door, on the inside. What a dick-head!'

This time, Addy tactfully said nothing though she did rather agree with him. It had lost him several minutes, no doubt.

'And then?'

'Then, of course, I let myself out of the museum, not locking any doors in case you had to run for it. I lingered for a moment in the porch, just to make sure none of the gang were around out the front keeping lookout or something, then ran like hell for the car.'

'Brill,' Addy said happily. 'And when you got to the station?'

'That's just the point I was trying to make about policemen never being around when you want them and always being around when you want to be alone. Before I could even reach the car, when I was still running across the pavement outside the museum, two enormous coppers made 'Hello-ello-ello' noises at me, grabbed me by both arms, and arrested me for breaking and entering,' Lance said bitterly. 'The stupid fools simply wouldn't listen when I tried to tell them what was happening in the kiln at the back of the museum. They just laughed when I said I worked there, and wouldn't even come back with me and go inside the building, just to take a look at the place. And when I told them you were in there they just made disbelieving noises and hauled me off to the station.'

'Oh, poor Lance!' Addy said. She wanted to giggle but it must have been awful at the time, she knew. 'So when you got to the station you explained to someone with a bit more clout . . .'

'No, not exactly. Not that I didn't try. . . I kicked up the most awful fuss . . . but Lord

Claverley from Felsham Hall had discovered some thieves actually in the act of taking his collection of impressionist paintings and everyone they could spare was sent off, hotfoot, to the Hall. So there was I stuck with these two thickoes and the desk sergeant who was already dealing with a couple of drunks and an old lady of a hundred or so who had come out for a walk in her nightie and forgotten who she was or where she came from . . . They were unhelpful, impatient and so stupid I could have smashed them, but in a way you could understand it.'

'Yes, I suppose,' Addy agreed. 'So what actually happened, Lance?'

'They telephoned the curator, Mr Williams, and he came round. He took hours and hours. I don't know what he was doing when the phone rang – I hesitate to think – but he was in a horrible mood by the time he did arrive. He barked that yes, I was employed by the museum, but not any more if I let myself in with my keys in the middle of the night . . . then I had to explain why I'd done it. I put on the sob-stuff good and thick, said your mother was ill in hospital, you had no relatives who could take you in, I'd offered you the shelter of my roof but it didn't seem quite right, somehow . . .' Lance rolled his eyes at her. 'That was the best thing I could have said; the old boy began to think I was a real little gent and to see my point of view, especially when I stressed that I'd not locked up afterwards, so you could get out, and that I was really afraid for you, because there were some villains carrying gold ingots out of the old kiln.'

'I've only seen him from a distance, but he

doesn't look a bad old boy. Did he believe you? Make the police take you there right away?'

It was silly, but despite the fact that she knew Lance had not got back in time, she wanted him to have had a chance of catching the men red-handed. But it was clearly not to be.

'I'd have done better not to mention the ingots or the villains at all, and just got myself out of it,' Lance admitted gloomily, passing a tractor towing an unwieldy trailer of hay as if neither of them existed. 'They just stopped believing me, like a light going out, and though I went back with them when they checked my story out, they had to be absolutely begged before they'd go across the courtyard and take a look at the old kiln.'

'Which was cleared of all traces, no doubt,' Addy said, sharing his misery. 'It's a wonder they didn't lock you up in a loony-bin or something.'

'Well, they didn't, because old Williams suddenly got ratty that there was no key on my bunch for the old kiln . . . said it was odd. So then he went up to his office and got out his keys, and he didn't have one either. By then the coppers were bored by the pair of us, thought us two credulous fools, but when old Williams told them to break the door down I think they cheered up quite a lot. I helped . . . It was good fun, I really put some beef into that door. I told myself it was Ned Armstrong's head I was thumping, and we got in after about twenty minutes of battering.'

'And then there was nothing?'

'Clean as a whistle. Except, of course, that it shouldn't have been. Just as they were coming out, with old Williams in a bloody awful mood by then because they'd found nothing, I said, 'But

138

if the place has been disused for years, sir, should it be so clean and well-swept?' and that stopped Williams in his tracks.

'We went back . . . he insisted. The coppers were dead fed-up with the whole thing by then and just wanted to get back to their nice station and their cocoa or whatever the fuzz put into their faces in the early hours. But old Williams just assumes everyone will do what he wants, and they did.

' "Someone's been here recently," the old boy said, bristling with annoyance. "Someone's been using a blowtorch . . . no, more likely oxy-acetylene equipment. . .look at those bricks." We couldn't see anything, the police and me, but the old boy swore there was fresh soot . . . anyway, at least they half believed me.'

'And did you find my drawing?'

'Yes . . . but not then. I had to leave when they did. They were so smug about everything, Addy! Because old Williams believed me they had to accept that someone had been in there and something was up, but when I told them you were missing I had to make the most awful fuss to get them to go back to your place, and then they weren't a bit bothered. Said you'd have made your way to a relative's place . . . Said you'd turn up all right for work in the morning and if you didn't that Mr Williams was to get in touch with them again.' They were approaching the suburbs of the town now and Lance had to slow down. 'Well, to cut a long story short it was what, about five o'clock, before we left the museum, and by eight thirty I was back, having spent the intervening hours scouring the town for signs of men or dogs or gold bullion.'

'Didn't you give their names?' Addy said suddenly. 'Why didn't the police go round to Ned Armstrong's, or Jacko's, or even to Mr Braithwaite's place?'

'I didn't see Mr Braithwaite; the only ones I recognized were Ned, and Jacko, but as soon as I used Ned's name I realized I'd made a mistake, because apparently he sometimes stays behind to open the kiln if they've been firing something they want fairly urgently. When I said I'd seen him, Mr Williams immediately said that Ned had a far better right to be in the yard late than I'd had, and we sort of went off at a tangent. And I don't think the coppers ever believed a word I'd said, not after thinking they'd caught a thief red-handed and being disappointed.'

'Well, will they believe now?' Addy said dubiously. 'I hate people thinking I'm a liar. What proof do we have?'

'A miner's hut full of gold that's too heavy to move in a hurry? A lorry with a load of villains all searching for you by now?'

'Yes . . . but will the police come to the hut with us? Or will they just fob us off again?'

'Not twice,' Lance said grimly. 'Not the pair of us they won't. Besides, the top brass should be in this morning – they'll listen.'

'Oh, and you didn't tell me when you saw my drawing and realized . . . you did find my drawing, didn't you?'

'Sure I did! As I was saying I went straight to the museum as soon as I dared, opened up and went through to the courtyard, then over to the old kiln. And there was this scrumpled bit of paper, to one side, near the bushes. Nothing else, no sign of a struggle or anything . . . so I picked up the paper and knew as soon as I'd smoothed it out where you were.'

'And you didn't take it back to the police?'

Lance snorted.

'Some chance! No way. I grabbed Betty and told her to tell Mr Williams where I'd gone, said to say it was dead important, and then rushed for the car. And came straight to the hut.'

'And found me already on my way out,' Addy said with satisfaction. 'Mind that woman!'

'She shouldn't cross the road at a crawl, looking in the other direction,' Lance said, swerving. 'Here's the police station. Get ready to be convincing!'

Despite their fears – and Addy was sure that Lance, too, was secretly doubtful if they would be believed – they had no trouble at all in persuading a certain Detective Inspector Johnson to take them seriously. Indeed, from the moment that Addy and Lance entered his office it was clear that this was a very different type of policeman from the two unimaginative, slow-thinking constables of the previous evening.

'I've read the report – the desk sergeant passed it to me,' he said as soon as they gave their names. 'So you've turned up,' he said to Addy. 'What's it all about, then?'

'I was kidnapped and dumped in an old hut on the moors,' Addy said succinctly. 'Can you come back there with us? The men who did it are still there, I think, or not far away.'

'Right.'

Detective Inspector Johnson clearly wasted few words. He picked up the phone, spoke into it, put it down sharply and then got to his feet, talking to them over his shoulder as he left the room.

'You know the way to this place? Right, explain in the car.'

It was odd how easy it was to explain clearly to someone who listened attentively, only putting in the odd word now and again to get you back on the track. Addy told her story, Lance told his, and by the time they had both finished the car was speeding along the road above the miner's hut.

'We turn right at the five-barred gate,' Lance said. 'From up here you can only see the roof of the hut but halfway down you'll see the lorry – if it's still there, that is.'

Halfway down they could see, and it was. The police car in which they had travelled was followed by a couple more but now their own vehicle slowed to a crawl, the faint purr of the engine sounding even lower than the crunch of the tyres over the rough ground.

'See anyone?' the detective inspector said as the hut came into view, with the lorry parked close, the back open, tailboard down.

'No. They'll be inside,' Addy said with certainty. 'Once they realized I'd gone, their next move would have to be to get the gold out of there.'

'True,' the inspector murmured. 'Then we'll park here, I think, and go down very quietly indeed – is there another way out of that hut?'

'Only the tunnel, and that's a dead end,' Lance said. 'Can we come with you, sir?'

'Wild horses wouldn't stop you,' the detective inspector said, grinning at them. 'Quietly, mind.'

Their car drew up without so much as a squeak, and the cars behind, warned by handsignals from the first driver, followed suit. Everyone got out and as they stole down towards the hut, walking on the grass rather than on the stony track, they saw that a Land Rover stood there as well as the lorry. Any approach would be entirely hidden from those inside the hut by the two vehicles.

As they got nearer, Lance and the inspector well to the fore, Addy heard the round and plummy tones of Mr Braithwaite. His voice was forceful, you could almost see the sweat that must be running down his plump cheeks.

'Get a move on! Get the stuff out of here! You don't think that girl's gone meekly home to Mummy, do you? She'll be straight to the cops before you can say "knife", but if they don't believe her, if we can lie low for a bit . . .'

Addy could see, by peering, that the lorry was over half-laden already but before she could say anything the police moved. They were all fairly large men, some uniformed and some not, but one moment they were grouped at the side of the lorry and the next they had fanned out, completely surrounding the front of the hut.

Inside, the men still moved the boxes, Mr Braithwaite's voice now rising . . . and a dog barked, sharply, from the Land Rover.

'Good day, gentlemen,' the inspector said, stepping into the men's line of vision, Addy and Lance close on his heels. 'Can we give you a hand with that? Just found it in the old mine, I dare say? Finders keepers, that sort of thing? Your own personal crock of gold – and out of a copper mine, too – quite astonishing! Simpson, Nicholls, just put these gentlemen into the cars so that we can have a word in the quiet of the station, will you?'

'There's nothing illegal about this gold,' Mr Braithwaite said, the plummy voice trembling a little. 'It's been paid for fair and square – if we choose to hide it away for a rainy day what's that got to do with anyone?'

'And kidnapping this young lady?'

'A joke,' someone said feebly. It was Jacko. 'Just a bit of a lark like, Inspector.'

'She's still laughing; but I'm not,' Detective Inspector Johnson said grimly. 'You can explain ever so much better in the station. Come along now, I'm sure you've got better things to do than bandying words with me. Step lively . . . my chaps will drive the lorry and the Land Rover.'

It was a bit of an anticlimax to find that Ringer wouldn't allow anyone to drive the Land Rover. 'He'll be a dead Ringer if he's left to bake in the jeep all day,' Lance remarked at one point, and Ned Armstrong, clearly agreeing with this, called the dog off at last and put him on a lead, whereupon Ringer beamed at everyone and voiced no objection to being bundled into the police car with his master and the rest of the men.

'I suppose it really is stolen gold?' Addy whispered to Lance during the bustle of getting the men out of the cars and into the police station. 'I suppose we haven't made a hideous mistake?'

Lance may well have had similar fears but presently, when the inspector joined them in his office, where he had sat them down whilst he dealt with the arrests, he reassured them.

'Men don't hide anything unless they've got a good reason to do so,' he said. 'Your friends are up to no good, even if they bought the gold and didn't steal it. We'll let you know as soon as we know ourselves but, right now, I suggest you get back to the pot-bank to reassure everyone that you're all right, and then go home and sleep the clock round. I imagine neither of you got much sleep last night.'

'I'll ring the hospital,' Addy said blearily to Lance, as he drew up outside her house. 'Not yet though, not until tonight.'

'Shall I come and pick you up, take you visiting?' Lance suggested. 'It's still very early. We'll be rested by, say, six o'clock.'

But Addy was too tired to care.

'No, it's all right, Lance. I'll ring the hospital from next-door's phone and explain. But thanks. See you in the morning.'

8

'Well, Mum, aren't you proud of me?' Addy said three days later, when she had settled her mother comfortably in the living-room with a tray bearing a welcome-home meal across her knees. 'Me and Lance foiled desperate robbers and saved the Government a lot of money. I'm glad you weren't too involved with that Jacko, though . . . Stan, I mean. We felt bad when we realized he was mixed up in it.'

'Easy come, easy go; I'll soon get another,' Mum said rather heartlessly. She poked with her spoon at the contents of a brandy glass on the tray. 'What's all this, then?'

'It's a prawn cocktail, as if you didn't know. You love them, you know you do. You often have one when a . . . a friend takes you out to dinner.'

'Oh, sure, but I never had one at home before,' her mother observed rather doubtfully. She dug her spoon into the mixture of prawns, sauce and salad, then spoke with her mouth full. 'It's good, love. Where did you learn how to make one?'

'From Lance's mum. When I said you were coming out of hospital she dreamed up a menu and told me how to make everything. She was

146

pleased as punch over us catching those crooks and there's a nice reward coming our way, the inspector told us.'

Mum sniffed and scraped her spoon vigorously round her glass to get the last smears of sauce.

'I wish you wouldn't keep talking about crooks and robbers, as though I'd been keeping company with a thief,' she said fretfully. 'They weren't crooks, not really. They bought the gold in Switzerland, all fair and square. I don't see anything wrong with buying foreign gold, if you've got the dough, that is.'

'Dough! That's old-fashioned talk, Mum, it's called readies now,' Addy said, smiling at her mother. 'I keep telling you, the crooked part came in because they smuggled the gold into Britain so they didn't have to pay VAT, but when they sold it they intended to charge VAT to the buyers. That was why they put it in the kiln and used the oxy-acetylene thing to take off the marks which would show that it was foreign gold. They'd have made an awfully big profit – millions, not thousands.'

'And fancy our Mr Braithwaite and Mr Singer from Export having enough money to buy all that gold!' Mum said. Her voice showed that she was far more awed by the men's ability to buy the gold than shocked at the swindle they had planned. Addy sighed. She really must make Mum see! It hurt her to realize that her mother thought that she, Addy, was being a bit mean to tell the police about a tax fraud; after all, everyone hates paying tax!

'It wasn't just them, Mum, it was a syndicate, a group of businessmen. And they borrowed most of the money, each of them borrowing what the bank would lend them . . . they invented a company, the inspector said, which they would just have dissolved after all the gold had been sold. So you see they were working a confidence trick and cheating the VAT people out of an enormous amount of revenue.'

'Revenue! There you are, you see, it was only a bit of a tax fiddle,' her mother said, seizing on the one word which seemed, to her, to vindicate the gold swindle. 'You could have kept your mouth shut, Addy!'

'No. You see, Mum, I'd seen them all, and I knew they were working some sort of a swindle. It sounds incredible, but I think they'd have had to get rid of me.'

'Get rid of you? What on earth do you mean? They tied you up, didn't they? Wasn't that enough? I thought they meant to untie you once they'd got away with the gold.'

'No, that couldn't have happened. They'd made no plans to leave, you see. Their wives and kids knew nothing, some of them had quite important jobs . . . you can't just split like that, on the spur of the moment, especially if just by silencing one girl you'd be in the clear.'

'Oh,' her mother said doubtfully. 'Well, it sounds more like the telly than life. What's next?'

'Can't you smell it cooking? Beef in a red wine sauce, mashed potatoes and peas. I'll go and fetch it through. And whilst you eat it, I'd like to have a bit of a chat about my future. Lance is coming round later – you still haven't met him, have you? – so I think we ought to get it over before then.'

Addy's mum, who had been craning towards the kitchen and the good smell of the stew, froze

148

she turned her face up towards her daughter's, suspicion in every pore.

'What's all this? Your future? I thought you'd be working in the paint-room for a few years and then you might come over to the big factory, work along of me.'

'We'll talk about it after I've dished up,' Addy said, making her escape into the kitchen. She and Lance had spent quite a lot of the last three days talking, and she had made up her mind that she might as well be happy as unhappy in her work. She would never settle in the paint-room, never . . . so why not take Lance's advice and just have a go at art college? It was one thing to discuss this happily with someone more or less her own age though, and quite another to prove to her mother that her change of heart was not the result of being brainwashed by Lance or over-impressed by his college status but, quite simply, the future she really wanted for herself. Or thought she wanted. She had been tempted, at first, to wait until Lance arrived so that they could tackle her mother together, but then when she thought about it further she realized that leaning on Lance in that way would never do. Her mother would be convinced that she, Addy, was being persuaded by a lad to go against her own flesh and blood. No, better that Addy and she discussed it and came to terms with it, and then if Lance talked about college and her mother was more or less in favour – well, resigned, then – she could ask him questions, sure of getting informed answers.

Addy drained the peas, began to spoon stew on to her mother's plate, and thought some more.

It was not just Lance who had persuaded her, but perhaps it had been his enthusiasm for her drawing which had made her actually take the step of getting in touch with her old art teacher to sound out the options open to her. And his stories of life at college were enough to make a cat laugh – but they had fun, he and his mates. What was more, from what her teacher had said, she thought she'd be on a lot more money once she did earn with a degree behind her than she'd ever make painting pots.

She was influenced by Lance in one way, though. She really liked him, wanted to see more of him, and the chances of him getting a job in the pot-bank next year were pretty remote. He wanted to travel – had suggested, in fact, that if she was going on to further education they might combine a travel-trip. She could sketch and paint, he said, whilst he did the languages bit and planned their route, booked accommodation and tickets and so on.

It sounded such fun, Addy thought yearningly, carrying her mother's plate back into the living-room. Actually learning about things like jewellery, silversmithing, dress design, still-life, portraits, stage-work . . . the list was endless and according to her teacher – and to Lance, who found some literature about it for her – she would have a chance to sample them all in her first year so that she could make up her mind what she wanted to do for the next three.

'There you are,' Addy said, standing the plate down on her mother's tray. She had put a lot of effort into the dish; boeuf bourgignon, Angela had called it, and had insisted that Addy buy tiny onions, button mushrooms and the best red wine she could afford. But her mother was looking at it as though it contained arsenic.

'What's the matter, Mum? Don't you like the look of it? It's awfully nice and the doctor said just to give you soft food for a few days, so I chose this.'

'I want to know what you and that Lance have been planning while I've been too ill to stop you,' her mother said slowly, poking her fork into the stewed beef. 'Just what's he been telling you about the paint-room not being good enough for you? Eh? After all, it was your idea to get work, I never forced you into it.'

'No, of course you didn't,' Addy said hastily. 'But let's be honest, Mum, I couldn't have afforded to go to college, it wouldn't have been fair to you. Only now I've got the reward money, and I really would like to go for an art degree, if they think I'm good enough.'

Her mother turned accusing eyes on her. She still had not touched her meal.

'After all I done for you? You'd just waltz off and leave me here alone? I can't manage to support you at college, chuck, and I don't suppose that reward money'd last long. I'm tired, if you want the truth. I'm not saying Jacko was a great lover but I'm not getting any younger and fellers will be harder to find as I get . . . get . . .'

She could not bring herself to say the word 'older', Addy realized. She felt very sorry for her mother all of a sudden, sitting huddled up in the chair, all her old ebullience drained away at the mention of Addy leaving home, and had to remind herself quite sharply of the way she herself had felt when Gran had first died and Mum had continued to go out night after night, leaving Addy to her own devices with cheerful disregard for her daughter's feelings.

'Look, it's not just a year or so, Mum, this is my whole future. If I get a degree I could get a really interesting job, well-paid too. Just let me tell you about it.'

'I won't change me mind,' Mum said crossly. She dug her fork into the stew and began to eat, at first idly and then with more enthusiasm.

'Well, first of all I can do a special course which is designed to show me, and my teachers, what particular form of art I'm best at. It's called a foundation course and for twelve months you do a bit of everything, fine art, dress design, graphics, photography and so on. At the end of that time if I'm good enough at one particular thing I can move on, go to a proper art college where they specialize in my subject and do a degree in whatever I've chosen. Imagine, Mum, it might be the Slade – your daughter at the Slade!'

'Cripes,' Mum said obligingly, but spoiled it by adding, 'What's the Slade?'

'It's a famous art college. But this foundation course is what you need to think about now, because that would be the first twelve months . . . I'd be doing silversmithing, book illustration, advertising . . .'

'That'll cost,' Mum said, as accusingly as though Addy had arranged it just to spite her. 'How'll we afford it, eh, with you not in work? You never thought of that!'

'Well, I might be able to get a grant, same as Lance does. If not I could work holidaytimes and evenings. I'd definitely get a grant if I could get into art college at the end of it, so it'd only be difficult for the first year. Also, Lance suggested I try and sell some of my paintings locally so that would help too . . . And then there's the reward . . .'

'If the Government's giving you the reward, you may be sure it won't amount to much. And I'm not sure you deserve much, giving blokes up to the law when all they were trying to do was better theirselves.'

It hurt; but it also made Addy angry. Why could her mother not see that the men had been greedy and callous? No wonder teenagers fought to leave home, when parental reactions were so weird. Not that all parents responded like that – Angela had been thrilled to bits with the whole thing and most complimentary about their earning the reward money. The trouble was, Mum simply wasn't using her head, she was just automatically against what she would have termed 'the bosses', and that included the VAT department.

'Mum, they were going to better themselves to the tune of nearly three million quid! And they were going to blow me out!'

Without altogether meaning to do so, Addy found she was shouting, but at least this got through to her mother, who put her knife and fork down almost regretfully.

'All right, all right, I dare say you did the best thing. Where would I be without you, love? That was a real lovely dinner.'

Mrs Bates smiled anxiously and Addy knew that she had heard herself, heard the unreasonableness of her argument and was sorry for it, sorry to have almost said she did not care if Addy had risked her life. But she wouldn't come right out and say it, not Mum!

'Thanks, but there's more to come. I'll go and fetch it.'

'A pudding, eh? By the way, what's the reward?'

Addy picked up the dirty dishes and named the reward. She was watching her mother's face at the time and got a good deal of satisfaction from the dropped jaw and bulging eyes. That would show Mum it could pay to be honest!

But her mother's logic was never quite like other people's.

'That much? Well, I reckon you've got a lot to thank those fellers for, my Stan amongst 'em! You'd never have got the reward if they hadn't nicked the stuff in the first place . . . mind, you'll only get half that, of course, but I bet your Lance is chuffed.'

Addy opened her mouth to explain that it would not be halved since Lance would get exactly the same, then shut it again. After all, the grateful Government was giving the money to her and she would use it wisely, to help with her education. But she could well imagine that her mother would want to tell her how to spend every penny, and her advice was unlikely to coincide with Addy's wishes. She was planning to buy some really striking, different clothes for the autumn. She had noticed that art students always led in the fashion field, so she didn't want to be thought dowdy and old-fashioned. And she had earmarked a strawberry-pink play-suit with white braces which would just suit Mum.

'So your mind's made up, then? You'll go to that college? Nothing I can say will stop you?'

'First it's the foundation course . . .' Addy began, but was stopped in mid-sentence.

'First? What do you mean?'

'Well, they run the foundation course here, at the local Tech. It's only after that . . .'

'Here? Oh, Addy, why on earth didn't you say so? If you're here for a whole year I'll have time to get used to the idea, make a few plans of me own. I can stand anything if you aren't buzzing off at once. Why, I might even get a lodger, just whilst you're away . . . a feller would be nice. Oh, a *year* . . . that's different!'

'So I can go ahead then?' Addy said, heading for the kitchen once more. 'Pudding's raspberry pie and cream. I made it.'

'If it's as good as that stew then it'll do me,' her mother said. 'When's that Lance coming?'

'Oh, in about half an hour. Why?'

'I'm looking forward to meeting him, that's why,' Mum said, raising her voice so that Addy could hear her even between the living-room and the kitchen. 'I want to see this feller who's actually made you interested in clothes, and cooking.'

'You'll like him,' Addy said, returning with the raspberry pie. 'I like him enormously.'

'Serious, are you? Making plans?'

'Only to enjoy myself with lots of people, lads and girls,' Addy assured her. 'I'm not getting married for years and years . . . centuries.'

Her mother bounced her curls with one hand and laughed in the old, carefree way.

'Oh, Addy, you're a chip off the old block after all,' she cried. 'You're going to break a score of hearts, just like your mum!'

Addy only smiled.

9

It was late afternoon, and it was the last day of work for Lance and Addy in the pot-bank museum.

Addy, grown slick at painting poppies, had finished work an hour before everyone else and said her goodbyes. Now she was ambling across the courtyard, to tell Lance that she was free to leave whenever he wanted to go.

They were having a last night out, because tomorrow Lance was off to visit his father for a long weekend and Addy intended to start work on a new picture for her portfolio. She still needed some life drawings and Mum had promised to sit for her and so had Di, so this weekend she would get those particular sketches out of the way.

But Lance, when she got to the museum, was behind the desk, selling picture postcards, mugs and commemorative plates, so Addy wandered past him and down the corridor, to the delft-room. She would miss the quiet of the museum, she reflected, when she was doing her foundation course, but she could come back here whenever she had time, and Mr Williams had promised that she could have a summer job next year, even if she did not fancy painting poppies for life.

The museum was closing now, so there was no one else in the long, white-painted rooms. Not even a lad with a broom, Addy thought, remembering the very first time she had met Lance. In the delft-room, it had been, where they had gone on that memorable night to see if they could see the ghost.

Thinking of the ghost made her remember that chase in the courtyard, and that made her spine give a little shudder, because quite soon after that particular event Ringer had attacked someone who had come to the Armstrongs' front door and had only just escaped being put down.

If it hadn't been for that little, straggly-haired thought, or imagining, it might have been me recovering in hospital, Addy told herself now, slipping into the delft-room and closing the door behind her. If it hadn't been for her, we might never have caught the gang because if Ringer had bitten me savagely I'd never have managed to climb up on to the roof. I might have died . . .

She walked slowly down the long room, glancing about her; the air felt heavy with the past, the shadows were growing longer, the sunlight no longer penetrated the high, blurred windows which overlooked the courtyard.

Addy closed her eyes. Something had helped her that night. Why should she be ashamed, in this quiet and lonely room, to admit it? She cleared her throat and spoke huskily, her eyes still closed.

'Are you there, little girl? Lance saw you once, or thought he did, and I almost saw you, that night in the courtyard. If you're here, I just wish you'd

158

show yourself. I want to say thank you, you s
By coming out and helping me that night you ve. y
probably saved my life.'

Her voice faltered to a stop; she hardly dared
to open her eyes, but when she did, the room was
still empty. Her gaze roved hopefully across the
pictures on the walls, the long, shining boards of
the floor, the glass cases with their mirror backs.

Nothing. No one. Only Addy's own reflection
in the backing mirror of the nearest case.

Addy sighed.

'Oh, all right. Perhaps I imagined you. Perhaps
Lance did . . . but Ringer didn't strike me as the
sort of dog to run away from nothing! Thanks
anyway, and goodbye.'

Addy turned away and was halfway back to
the door when she froze, the hair on the back of
her neck prickling erect, her skin goose-fleshing.

She might have smiled at her own reflection
as she turned away, of course she might have,
easily.

But she had not waved. She knew she had
not waved.

And the reflection in the mirror, dimly seen in
the gathering dusk, had raised a hand in farewell
as she had said goodbye.

THE END

If you would like to receive a Newsletter about our new Children's books, just fill in the coupon below with your name and address (or copy it onto a separate piece of paper if you don't want to spoil your book) and send it to:

The Children's Books Editor
Transworld Publishers Ltd.
61–63 Uxbridge Road
Ealing
London W5 5SA

Please send me a Children's Newsletter:

Name: ....

Address: ....

....

....

All Children's Books are available at your bookshop or news-agent, or can be ordered from the following address:
Transworld Publishers Ltd.
Cash Sales Department,
P.O. Box 11, Falmouth, Cornwall TR10 9EN

Please send a cheque or postal order (no currency) and allow 80p for postage and packing for the first book plus 20p for each additional book ordered up to a maximum charge of £2.00 in UK.

B.F.P.O. customers please allow 80p for the first book and 20p for each additional book.

Overseas customers, including Eire, please allow £1.50 for postage and packing for the first book, £1.00 for the second book, and 30p for each subsequent title ordered.